Apocalypse

The Wasteland Chronicles, Volume 1

by Kyle West

Published by Kyle West, 2012.

This is a work of fiction. Similarities to real people, places, or events are entirely coincidental.

APOCALYPSE

First edition. December 5, 2012.

Copyright © 2012 Kyle West.

Written by Kyle West.

10 9 8 7 6 5 4 3 2 1

Also by Kyle West

The Wasteland Chronicles
Apocalypse
Origins
Evolution

Watch for more at kylewestwriter.wordpress.com.

For Dad: Thanks for the read and advice; not just in books, but in life.

Prologue

The world ended on December 3, 2030, with the impact of the meteor Ragnarok in the American heartland. When the world ended, a new one began – one which over ninety nine percent of humanity did not live to see.

Most did not die in the impact, but in the weeks following it. The fallout clouded the skies, shielding most sunlight. As infrastructures collapsed, billions died from lack of food, medication, and shelter. Violence and gangs arose from the dust, skirmishing for control of limited supplies. Within a few years, only a tiny fraction of the world's population remained.

The meteor fallout sent global temperatures plummeting. Summer was the new winter, and winter was Antarctic death. Those living in far northern or southern climes could do nothing but perish as the extreme cold snapped power lines and destroyed generators. Even in places as far south as California, it was not uncommon for someone to freeze to death in the summertime.

What followed was a mass extinction event not seen since the Great Dying of the Permian and Triassic Periods over 250 million years ago. The age of humans was over. Maybe, the age of intelligent, complex life was over.

Ragnarok had not been catalogued by any astronomical organization, including the Near-Earth Object Program funded by NASA, and apparently was completely missed. It was discovered in November of 2020, and collision with Earth was predicted with near 100 percent accuracy. Dark Day, as it came to be called, was to come December 3, 2030.

The United States and a pact of eighty nations pooled resources to divert the course of Ragnarok. After much deliberation, it was decided that a manned spacecraft would be constructed and shot to the asteroid, where it would attach rockets that would push Ragnarok away from Earth.

The plan, at first, seemed to succeed. But for reasons unknown to this day, Ragnarok resumed its former course.

Two other attempts were made. One mission was lost en route. The last mission, hastily put together and launched in 2028, made it to Ragnarok. However, the rockets that were to push Ragnarok off course malfunctioned.

After this final failure, the window to change Ragnarok's course had passed. Impact was inevitable.

From 2020-2030, the U.S. government constructed 144 Bunkers in twelve districts throughout its territory. Only the highest ranking government officials were allowed inside the Bunkers, along with the wealthy who could finance them, and the intelligent who could man them. The Bunkers collectively contained room for thousands of people, and spanned miles underground. Each was self-sufficient, with recycling centers, dormitories, recreation facilities, medical bays, hydroponics, and everything else needed to sustain large populations for an indefinite length of time. The plan was, when the dust settled, citizens could reemerge and rebuild.

But life in the Bunkers was fraught with unseen complications. Disease, mutiny, and internal breakdowns took the Bunkers, one by one. Surface survivors, called Wastelanders by underground citizens, overran the Bunkers out of desperation for shelter and supplies if their locations were discovered.

Thirty years following the impact of Ragnarok, only four Bunkers remained operational. One Bunker, designated Bunker 108, was sheltered within the slopes of the San Bernardino

Mountains, about a hundred miles east of Los Angeles.

By 2060, small communities had formed in the American West and California. Los Angeles had a population of ten thousand. But as the local population grew, Bunker 108 quietly continued to operate, keeping its location secret so as not to become a target of Wasteland raiders. Bunker 108 never let anyone in – or out – except those on official government business.

However, Bunker 108 could not keep the world out forever.

Chapter 1

When a citizen of Bunker 108 turns sixteen, he or she is deemed old enough to start reconnoitering.

Reconnoitering is dangerous work – not so much because of the Wastelander bogeymen that kept me up at night as a kid. There are a ton of ways to die out there – windstorms and cold not being the least of them.

Always, when you go out of Bunker 108, you never know if you are coming back.

Michael Sanchez drew lots with me that day. Michael was a seasoned vet, all hard muscle, and an officer to boot. I looked like a pencil in comparison – five foot seven, and one hundred twenty seven pounds. We were quite the pair as we walked out the entrance door, down the long tunnel to the exit of Bunker 108.

I was nervous as hell. I had never been allowed into the Waste before. Not until now.

Yesterday had been my sixteenth birthday.

As we walked, I felt like I was in a dream – or a nightmare – I wasn't sure which.

I just hoped I didn't have to use my rifle, even though I knew how. Everyone was required an hour's practice each week at the firing range, minimum. Chief Security Officer Chan wanted everyone ready – for what, I didn't know. We were told Wastelanders would kill for anything.

So, we had orders to kill them first.

Conflicts with Wastelanders are rare. But Chan likes to keep a close eye on things. A "kill first" policy prevents anyone from running away and letting others know that we're here.

That was what I was most nervous about – not the cold dry wind, the dead world, the red hazy sky stretching above, or the lack of sun dimmed by layers of meteor fallout. No – I was scared that we would find someone, and I would have to shoot him.

We were now at the door. Large bold numbers, 108, were pressed into the thick metal. For my entire sixteen years, that door has served as the barrier between safety and danger, known and unknown, fake and real. And now, I was about to go outside for the first time in my life.

Michael, the person I was partnered with, was twenty-four: tall, good-looking, with coppery skin. He went to the sun rooms often. Officers were allowed longer light baths than civilians. Officers had other perks and signs of status: cushier apartments, more meal credits, and more days off. Chan did everything to incentivize the people who kept him in power. Everyone wanted to be an officer.

Michael twisted the wheel, his muscles bulging beneath his desert camo. It was colder and drier out here in the entrance tunnel. I hopped up and down a few times, trying to get some blood flowing. I felt my own desert camo hoodie bounce up and down on my head. The cold had killed a recon caught in a dust storm, two years ago. It never paid to be too careful.

The wheel groaned as it gave, little by little. Finally, Michael opened it with a clang. He pulled it slowly inward until the Wasteland outside was revealed.

The natural light, though dim, still blinded me. A cold rush of dry wind met my face. I raised my hand to shelter my eyes from dust. As my eyes adjusted, I could first make out distant red mountains, like upside-down, bloody teeth. Then, before them were crimson dunes that looked like they belonged on Mars rather than Earth. A dilapidated, rusted crane laid half-buried maybe half a klick out, where it had been since December 3, 2030 – Dark Day, the day where most of humanity, and most of life, died.

"Welcome," Michael said with a sardonic grin, "to the Wasteland."

***

I followed Michael down the gravelly slopes of Hart Mountain. I pulled my hoodie far over my head to keep out the cold as best I could. It was late September, and got below freezing every night.

Though I had seen countless pictures of the Waste before, I could not help but take it in with numb shock. All vegetation was short, squat, clinging for life in the sandy, cracked earth. Everything was dead – truly dead. What life there was had left long ago. I often imagined Old Cali, like in the movies I watched in the digital archive. I dreamed of a hot, sandy beach, the blue ocean and sky, the bright, heavenly sun without a cloud to bar its light. I loved watching those movies, and would spend hours in the archive living in a dream world and wishing I had been born a hundred years ago, and not 2044.

We had been walking five minutes when Michael spoke.

"You're quiet, Alex," he said. "I thought you'd be excited about your first recon. Some luck to draw lots the day after your birthday."

I didn't respond. Michael fell into silence.

He was right. I didn't talk much. I didn't see the point. I don't really know why I'm like this – it's just always been this way. Well, not always. I've seen a lot of death. It started with my mom, when I was seven. Then my little sister, also when I was seven. My mom had been giving birth. In a harsh world, death comes often.

We were out of sight from home by now. I shivered as a particularly chilly wind blew. We passed a metallic trailer, shimmering in the late afternoon haze.

"That trailer's for dust storms," Michael said. "You never want to be caught in one. It will be the last mistake you make."

We stopped in front of the trailer. Michael paused.

"Let's wheel around the mountain," he said. "We're taking the long route today."

"What's the long route?"

"Finally, some goddamned curiosity. The long route goes all the way around Hart Mountain. It's about a five mile course, total."

He walked on. Michael was alright, for an officer. He had a wife and a kid. Like me, he had never seen Old Earth.

My father had. When he was ten, the government had put him and his dad, my grandfather, in Bunker 108. My grandfather, Lorin Keener, was a brilliant immunologist. The government only took the brightest, the highest-ups, and the people with the fattest wallets into the Bunkers. I hate to think of all those people who died, but in the end, I guess it comes down to whoever writes the largest check or has the biggest brain or the prettiest face. Well over 99.9 percent of the nation was left to fend for itself when Meteor crashed down.

The ones who survived are called Wastelanders, and we do what we can to avoid them, and to keep *them* avoiding *us*.

Wastelanders aren't like us citizens. For one, there are more of them. They are violent, brutal, barbaric, and do anything they can to survive. They are like animals, and they kill not just for supplies, but for fun. There have been several deaths during my life due to Wastelanders – men lost on recons, their bodies found later, half-buried in red sand. Sometimes, when raiders camped too close, Chan would order them eliminated in the dead of night. Losses sometimes happened.

The U.S. left the Dark Decade with one hundred and forty four Bunkers. Some didn't survive due to internal breakdowns, sure. But some were overrun by scared, starving people who wanted the huge stash of food and supplies the Bunkers held. Now, in the year 2060, only four Bunkers are left: Bunker 76, Bunker 88, Bunker 108, and Bunker 114. Bunker 114 is not far from ours – maybe fifty miles. It's sheer luck that it's so close and still running. During the Dark Decade, a lot of Bunkers were built in the Mojave because of nearby L.A., San Diego, and Vegas.

If there is a reason for secrecy beyond safety, I don't know it. I know we are a center of xenobiological research, which might be important enough to keep the location under wraps. If such research were seized or destroyed, it would completely frustrate our efforts to understand what is going on at the Ragnarok impact site, nearly a thousand miles away in Nebraska and Wyoming.

I'm glad I'm a citizen, living in a Bunker. We have warm beds, hot showers, and a safe life. Bunker 108 has a digital archive where millions of books, recordings, and movies are stored. I spend a lot of my off time there, listening to the music of the Old World, watching the movies, reading the books. We have a commons with a pool and a basketball court, among other amenities, including the sun room – fifteen minutes of pure, lighted bliss, giving all Bunker residents their daily dose of Vitamin D. Everything is warm, everything is in its right place, and people are happy – for the most part.

Right now, Bunker 108 has a population of four hundred, and is run by Chief Security Officer Chan. He's a little harsh, but he keeps things in order. I just try to dodge him when he walks the corridors.

Michael and I arrived at the north face of Hart Mountain. As we walked I stared at the distant, red peaks. I was used to the confines of the Bunker, and seeing so much open space was surreal.

"Jesus ..." Michael said.

I stopped short. "What?"

Face down in front of us, hidden by some wispy scrub, lay the body of a man, stabbed several times in the back. Small traces of purple slime oozed from the wounds. He wasn't moving.

Michael knelt beside the man, placing a hand on his neck.

"There's a pulse," Michael said.

I wondered why Michael was checking for a pulse, and not shooting him. That was standard protocol: if you found a Wastelander, you killed him, end of story. But after looking at what the man was wearing, I saw why.

The number 114 was emblazoned on the sleeve.

"Is he from that other Bunker?" I asked.

For some reason, my eyes drifted up, focusing on a distant boulder. Something was off about it.

Then I realized what it was. A woman's face was peeking around its side.

Chapter 2

I knew exactly what I was supposed to do – tell Michael about the woman, and have her eliminated.

It was so simple, yet I didn't open my mouth. She was a Wastelander. A *real* one. She could tell people where she saw us, and the entire security of Bunker 108 could be compromised.

She might have been the one to stab the man in the first place.

Yet I didn't say a word. I just stared out there at that giant red rock as the evening's shadows stretched, feeling like an idiot. By now, the woman had long disappeared. I wasn't even sure if she had been there. I could only remember her face, pretty, even with the distance, framed by long, black hair.

Was it only my imagination?

Michael's voice snapped me back to attention.

"Alpha Patrol to Base – do you copy, over?"

"Base to Alpha Patrol, what is your status, over?"

"We found a man, stabbed several times in the back. He's unconscious, but there is a pulse. I think he's from that other Bunker, over."

The handheld radio went quiet. I took my attention off the boulder, and looked at the man. Those sharp blue eyes that stared upward had held thoughts, once. Now, they held nothing.

Why was he here? Why had he been killed?

"If he's from Bunker 114, what's he doing out here?" I asked.

He had to be here for a very important reason. Officer Chan would be most interested in this.

The radio crackled to life.

"Alpha Patrol, what is your location, over?"

"Two miles onto the long route, over."

"Can you give a description of the man, over?"

"Male. Age: 35-45 years. Ethnicity: white. Short of stature, with black hair. He carries nothing – no ID, no gun, no pack. God knows how he made it this far." Michael sighed. "He may have been murdered and robbed. There are three deep stab wounds in the back – one on the lower right back side, and two more to the left of the spine. Each of them has blood and dark pus oozing through his clothes, over."

The wind blew cold and dry, covering the man's pale face in a thin layer of red dust. The sun faded behind hazy clouds above the distant red mountains. It was now night. It was high time to get back.

"Alpha Patrol," said a voice, icy and clear. It was CSO Chan. "We're sending a team to transport the man to base. If he came from 114, it must have been for an important reason. Remain where you are, and keep an eye out for hostiles. There may be raiders in the area. Do you copy, over?"

"Copy that," Michael said.

"Good. Over and out."

I watched where I had seen the woman. The boulder became shrouded in shadow as the dim sun dipped below the western mountains. She was long gone by now – if she knew what was good for her.

For some reason, I felt pointing her out would have been wrong. Maybe I'm soft. Maybe if it had been a man instead, I would have felt differently. Yet, no matter how I rationalized my decision, I couldn't make the sick feeling in my gut go away.

The cold wind never abated, blowing on my already numb face, stinging me with shards of sand, cracking my lips dry. At long last, flashlights crested the rise behind us. Voices signaled the arrival of reinforcements.

Four men approached, their faces lost to darkness.

"Where is he?" the one in charge asked, whose voice I didn't recognize.

"Down here," Michael said.

Two men pointed their guns into the darkness. Everyone else, myself included, lifted the body, one person per limb. Together, we lugged the man back to base.

Michael explained everything on the way, but I kept silent. I was thinking of the woman. They asked me several questions about what happened. I answered in monosyllables, echoing everything Michael had already said. There was no use in saying anything about the woman now. If I did, I would be severely disciplined, at best, for not speaking up earlier. At worst...I didn't want to think about that. Now that I was sixteen, I could be tried as an adult, and the holding cells in the Officers' Wing were mighty small.

When we reached the vaulted door of Bunker 108, I felt intense relief. The outside of the door, though metallic, was the same dull brown as the terrain. Unless you were right up on it, it was almost indistinguishable from the mountainside.

The door was opened from the inside, revealing an officer. We stepped inside Bunker 108 as the officer shut the door and twisted it shut behind us.

We were safe. I had finished my first recon, but for good reason, I didn't feel all that proud.

Lights in the entrance tunnel flashed on overhead, revealing the six of us carrying our burden inside. We left the rocky tunnel and entered the atrium. The receptionist's desk was empty – Deborah had either gone home, or was at the caf.

Next to the half circular desk stood my father, Steven Keener, waiting with a gurney and a nervous orderly at his side.

My father was thirty eight years old. His brown hair, always disheveled, was streaked with gray. Dark circles underlined his hazel eyes, giving him the appearance that he hadn't slept in days.

He shot me a worried glance as we put the man on the gurney.

"Dad..."

"Not now, son. Go eat. We will speak later."

My father and the orderly started wheeling the patient toward the medical bay, flanked by the officers.

My father was always busy. Between his duties as senior doctor and his own pet project of researching the xenovirus, it was hard to find time with him. He sometimes put in over a hundred hours a week at the lab, all while caring for patients. I didn't see how it is possible.

After handing off my rifle to the quartermaster (a small armory was kept near the front desk), I headed to the commons to kill time before dinner. In the corner, several officers and a few civilian women were watching a movie on the big screen. A couple of kids were playing ping pong in the corner. I sat in a chair in another corner, and watched some of my classmates play basketball.

In a community of about four hundred people, you know everyone, and everyone knows you. Not enough to be your friend, per se, but enough to have a sense of who you are, who your friends are, and what you are about. It's hard for me to imagine what life was like in the cities – like old L.A., where the population was in the millions. A world where you didn't know everybody seemed strange and scary to me. Maybe it was for them, too. Only a few in the Bunker remember those times well. Most of the old are gone. A lot went crazy, living underground – or so I've heard. But I've never heard of anyone born underground who went crazy.

I don't think it's that bad. I have the archive, and someday, I will be a doctor here, too, like my dad. Maybe even sit on the Citizens Council like him, though he rarely attends because of his duties.

I am no one special – scrawny, quiet, and a little too smart for my own good. That's what my dad says, anyway – that last bit, not the scrawny and quiet thing. My goal: to exist and survive, and not get in the way. When you get in the way, other people make trouble for you. There is only one true friend I can claim, and her name is Khloe. We've known each other from the cradle, but we have been distancing lately. I don't know if it's us just getting older or whether it's because she's hanging with a different group.

I reached for my sketchbook in my pack. Drawing is one of my ways to blow off steam, and I have a knack for it. As I sat in my chair, I just let the pencil move, not really paying attention to what it created. Ten minutes later, without realizing it, I had finished a sketch of the woman I had seen, as I had remembered her. Her face was slightly shaded – I remember an olive complexion, black, silky hair, and pretty, almond eyes. I was amazed by the amount of detail I remembered, but much of it was probably my imagination. She had been pretty far away.

It was the face of a woman who may have killed someone. It was a person I might have had killed. Now, I was drawing her.

I ripped the sketch out, tearing it to pieces. I felt my heart race for no good reason – like someone was going to see the sketch and know exactly what happened. I looked up to see that everyone was leaving the commons, heading for the caf.

I wondered what was happening in the medical bay – the stabbed man, my father, and even what Chief Security Officer Chan was doing.

But he wouldn't know about *her*.

I got up, and headed for the caf.

Chapter 3

I ate alone at mess. My thoughts were heavy, and I just couldn't get into any sort of conversation.

People walked by, their faces questioning. Word had gotten around that something had happened out there. I ate my potatoes and vegetables in silence, never looking up.

"Sitting by yourself. As usual."

A pretty, black-haired girl plopped on the metal bench next to me.

"Khloe. What are you up to?"

"Just hanging out, I guess. Eating some food, as I'm wont to do. You?"

"Much the same."

I took another bite. I could feel her staring at me.

"So..." she asked. "How was it?"

I swallowed. "What do you mean?"

"Don't play coy with me, Alex Keener. I know you came across a dead body."

"Right to the point, huh?"

"I'm a busy girl. So what happened?"

"Well, he wasn't quite dead, actually. He's in the medical bay with my dad. Three stab wounds." I ate another mouthful of food, and swallowed. "It was pretty bad."

"Yeah, I know that much. Who is he? Where did he come from?"

"I don't know. If anyone does, it's Sanchez or Chan, or...what's with all these questions, anyway?"

She smiled. "You know me. I'm curious."

"I'm sorry," I said. "If you've been asking around, you probably know more than me."

She laughed. "Yeah. Right. Well, if you're not saying anything, you must be hiding *something*."

I couldn't help widening my eyes a little.

"Hit the nail on the head, huh?"

"Yeah, maybe a little."

"Well, what happened? Spill the beans."

"Nothing happened. We went out, found the body, and called for help...now we're here. Eating beans."

I looked at her and smiled, but she was still not convinced.

"Funny," she said. "I'm not letting you off that easy. Alex, how long have we known each other?"

"Oh no, not this..."

"Yeah, a long time. Our whole lives. And who would you say your best friend is?"

"I don't have to answer that..."

"I want to hear it, anyway."

"You, of course."

"Okay," she said. "Something's bugging you, and I'm going to pry it out of you if it's the last thing I do. You saw something weird. And *you're* going to tell me. I thought we were friends."

I didn't answer for a while. It wasn't that I didn't trust her. I knew she would keep a secret. But what I had seen weighed on me, and it would not be fair to lay it on her. What if she got in trouble, too?

"Still not talking, huh? Whatever happened, you can't pen it up inside. You need someone to talk with. I'm here."

"You're persistent, aren't you?"

She shrugged. "I know you, Alex. You're too quiet. It's okay to let your feelings out. Really, it would be good for you."

I was about to protest the "feelings" bit, but decided it wasn't worth it. "Maybe later on. Somewhere more quiet than here."

"Fine. The chapel, at twenty hundred?"

I smirked. "Are you sure this is just swapping secrets?"

She rolled her eyes. "Yeah. I'm sure."

"Geez, only kidding."

"Finally, I get some time with you. Now that you're reconnoitering and everything, I guess you're too cool for me."

"Khloe, you know that's..."

"Hey," Khloe said, touching my arm. "It'll be fine, whatever it is. Just trust me."

I looked at her for a second, trying not to focus on how good her hand felt on my arm. I stopped trying to figure her out years ago. There were feelings there, at least on my part. For some reason, nothing had ever materialized. She always seemed to be with some other loser.

Okay, maybe that was a bit harsh. All the same, I did always find myself being just the friend. Honestly, that that was part of the reason for our distance, lately. It hurt to be around her.

"Alright. I'll meet you there."

Khloe smiled. "Good." She jumped up, and half turned from me. "Twenty hundred, the chapel. That's almost two hours away, so be ready."

Khloe went back to her table, and I went back to my food. I didn't know if I had made the right choice. But I knew Khloe – if she knew something was bothering me, she wouldn't let up until I told her.

Who knew? Maybe telling her would get it off my chest.

Maybe.

Chapter 4

After dinner, I went to the medical bay, entering the double doors. There were four operating tables, one set up in each quadrant of the room, all empty. The mystery man wasn't here, so I knew he was in the back room, which was used for the extreme cases.

The air was cold, and stank of medicine. It chilled me as I walked across the bay, my boots sticking to the gray linoleum floor. I never really liked this place. It felt soulless and bare, and was colder than the rest of the Bunker.

The door to my dad's office in the back left corner was open, which meant he was in. I went inside, and found him alone at his desk. He squinted with bespectacled eyes at his computer screen, his lab coat wrinkled and dirty.

He gave a small, tired smile.

"Alex..."

"You missed dinner."

"Oh." My father frowned. It was as if he had forgotten that this thing called "dinner" existed. "That's funny. I'm not even hungry."

"It's alright. How is he? And *who* is he?"

"Not good. He's not dead, but he is dying. And as far as *who* he is...we don't know. Not yet, anyway. Comm lines with Bunker 114 are still down, as they have been for the past few days."

This was not a warning sign in and of itself. Communication with Bunker 114 has always been spotty, especially recently.

"Did you stay up all night again?" I asked.

He didn't answer that question. "I'm getting close, Alex. Very close. And this man might just have the key I'm looking for."

"What do you mean?"

"The xenovirus." My dad looked up at me. The tiredness was gone, and the energy had returned to his eyes. "I might be able to finally figure out how the damn thing works, Black Files or not."

This wasn't the first time for my dad to mention the Black Files. The Black Files are years of collective research on the xenovirus, archived in Bunker One, in Cheyenne Mountain, Colorado. Though many scientists worked on the project, it is the brainchild of Dr. Cornelius Ashton. It documents the xenovirus from its first discovery in the 2030's, its various strains, and the flora it affects. The xenovirus first appeared at the Ragnarok impact site thirty years ago, suggesting it came from the meteor itself. From the crater came a strange, yet probably harmless, growth known as "xenofungus" – an organic swath of pink, purple, and orange that covers the ground and seems to thrive in any environment. Certain strains of the xenovirus also affect Earth plants. These plants, once infected, become twisted and live in symbiosis with the xenofungus. Areas taken over by the xenofungus and twisted plants are known as "Blights." None exist as far west as California, though they are common in the middle of the United States, which is closer to Ragnarok Crater.

My father, as well as a team of scientists at Bunker 114, are researching the xenovirus, hoping to discover how it works. My dad, in particular, is looking for a way to eradicate it within plant species – to cure it, if you will. My father believes the Black Files, if ever uncovered, might be the key to aiding his research.

There is only one problem: Bunker One disappeared overnight twelve years and is presumed offline – which means the Black Files are also inaccessible. To this day, no one knows what happened. The main theory is that the xenovirus infected the farms of Bunker One, causing all the food to become inedible. If this happened, then everyone there would have starved. But it begs the question: why didn't Bunker One seek help from nearby Bunkers? And why wouldn't they have told anyone? Whatever happened, there were no survivors. To this day, every expedition sent there has never returned. Our Bunker never sent anyone there, but other Bunkers have. Those Bunkers are gone now, too.

In any case, the Black Files are in Bunker One, locked away in what is probably an underground tomb.

My father thought the xenovirus was a byproduct of natural evolution. He said that mass extinction events, similar to the Ragnarok Extinction, stimulated a huge growth in biodiversity over the long run. He believed the xenovirus was the beginning of that growth – that it was life's way of surviving given conditions of the meteor fallout, constant cold, and lack of water, as it seems perfectly adapted to Earth's current climate.

The xenovirus isn't a virus, really, but the name has stuck. It is an agent that attaches itself to DNA, copies it, and transposes it onto other life forms. The xenovirus mixes and matches genes of different plant species until it creates something completely new. It does this at random, as if trying to guess what might work. It's hard to imagine how such a complicated life form arose so quickly, but my dad believes it is possible if there enough environmental stressors. The xenovirus is so one of a kind that my dad thinks it should be classified in its own kingdom.

To me, I think the xenovirus is creepy. Watching the lab samples of xenofungus makes my skin crawl. There is something sinister about how fast it grows and swallows plants, sometimes overnight. It creates this pinkish goo that does not really have a name. My dad and I just call it "slime," at least until we can think of something more creative.

"I ran tests on this man's blood" my father said. "It's full of microbes infected with the xenovirus. These microbes, in turn, are making him sick."

"I thought the xenovirus wasn't supposed to affect people."

"The xenovirus isn't infecting him directly. It's infecting the microbes in his bloodstream, and these infected microbes are doing a number on him. One thing is clear; it is killing him. The injuries I could have fixed. But against this infection, I have nothing. He is hanging on by a thread. If nothing else, I hope having him here will give me some answers."

"Is he contagious?"

"As long as you did not touch any infected areas, you should have nothing to fear. All the same, he is quarantined."

All of a sudden, I felt sick with dread. *Had* I touched any infected areas? There might have been a point, as we were picking him up, when one of the wounds brushed my clothes. Other than that, I had just held the guy's lower leg.

"I don't think I got anything on me."

"Good." My dad stared at the top of his desk, his eyes hazy.

"Get some sleep," I said. "You won't figure anything out if you're tired."

"Yes," he said. "I know. But I have to run some more tests. I'm the only one with the expertise to solve this. Who knows? If I hurry, maybe the patient's life might be saved."

"I just wonder who he is," I said, "and what he had to tell us. It must have been important."

"If Chan has found out anything from Bunker 114, he hasn't let me know."

"He couldn't have been out there for no reason..."

My father smiled. "You are curious, Alex. Maybe too much for your own good."

"Now, what is *that* supposed to mean?"

"It means keep your nose out of trouble."

The problem was, I had already run into trouble. I thought of the woman. For all I knew, she was halfway to L.A., with plans to tell everyone where we were. Okay, that was a worst case scenario.

However, what I knew weighed on me terribly.

I had to tell someone. If I couldn't tell my dad, who could I tell?

"This guy wasn't alone, Dad. There was a woman, not far away hiding behind a rock. I was the only one who saw her. She might have tried to kill him. She might have been with him at the time, I don't know. I didn't tell anyone. I just...froze. She ducked away, and is probably far from 108 by now."

My father frowned. Instead of being angry, he looked contemplative – like he had received a new piece of the puzzle.

"Hmm. Maybe she *did* do it. Well, whatever happened, we have no control over it now. She is gone, and even if you had told, she would be dead. Neither would have been of use to me."

"You won't tell, right?"

My father smiled. "Alex, of course not. I'm your father. I'm on your side, no matter what. You did the right thing."

Even with his approval, I wasn't sure. I sighed. "I hope so."

At that moment, Chief Security Officer Chan entered the medical bay. He was the absolute last person I wanted to see. He was short, of Chinese descent, and had cropped, gray hair. His face was placid, betraying no emotion. I knew he often practiced meditation, as well as martial arts. He inspired as much fear as he did respect. Every part of his body was hard lines and angles, without a trace of fat.

He wasted no time in addressing me.

"I need to speak with your father alone, Alex," he said.

"Yes, Officer Chan."

I glanced at my father. He nodded, urging me to follow Chan's direction.

I walked out of the bay and into the corridor, feeling Chan's gaze douse me like ice water. Of course, Chan would be interested in the man's progress. He would not miss this for anything. As Chief Security Officer of Bunker 108, it was his job not to miss things.

The man had clearly been heading here. But why? What message did he carry from 114, and why was Chan so interested in it?

In the Old World, Chan was an intelligence officer. When he entered Bunker 108, he was in his early thirties. Now in his sixties, he was one of the few old ones left. As the higher-ups died or were relocated, Chan slowly took firmer hold on the operations here. He has been in charge almost my whole life, so I don't remember a time where he wasn't. Though strict – maybe even draconian – there was no question: Chan has kept us safe all these years, and he is the main reason why we are one of four Bunkers left, when one hundred and forty four started out.

I walked down the corridor. The hallway was empty right now; most people would be in the commons, the archive, or home in their apartments. I walked past the caf, where the kitchen staff was wiping down tables.

As I rounded the corner, I could see at the end of the hall two wooden, double doors with stained glass windows. I headed there, trying to suppress my worry for my father.

I knew he probably wouldn't be sleeping tonight, either.

Chapter 5

I walked into the chapel. It was dark; the only lighting was from the hallway, and the air was thick and musty. Ten rows of pews lined the red-carpeted center aisle, which led to a low stage and communion rail. Being in this small sanctuary with the old familiar smell of wood and books made me think of younger days.

Khloe was already waiting in one of the back right pews. She was tapping her foot and leafing through a hymnal.

She looked up as I approached.

"There you are," she said. "I was beginning to worry you'd stand me up."

"You? Never."

"Sit down."

I took my place beside her. She put the hymnal up.

"It's so dark in here," I said.

"Yeah," she said. "No one really comes here anymore."

This place was once a center for the Bunker. Then Father Nielsen died. Every Sunday, he preached. Almost everyone would gather to hear his words. My dad was one of the few who didn't. He never put much stock in religion, and I guess he rubbed off on me a bit, all the more so as I've grown older.

Those had been different times. Then, Father Nielsen got cancer. Even my dad couldn't save him from that.

With Father Nielson's death came the death of the church, slowly. Some tried take his place, but no one spoke with his conviction.

Father Nielson had been dead two years, and it showed. Dust coated the hymnals in the pews. Cobwebs stretched from ceiling to floor in the dark corners, hanging from the hanging Christ on his cross. I tried not to notice how defeated He looked.

I was the one to break the silence.

"I saw someone, out there."

Khloe stared at me blankly. "You mean someone other than the guy you found?"

I nodded. "Yeah. A woman was watching from behind a rock. She ducked away fast, but I'm sure I saw her. I was the only one to notice. I even drew a picture of her."

"Can I see it?"

I shook my head. "I tore it up."

Khloe sighed. "So, that's what's been bothering you?"

"You say it like it's not a big deal."

"No...it is."

"I don't know what to do. I don't know why I didn't say anything to Michael about it."

I trailed off. My words died on the dark walls. I waited for Khloe to say something.

"I just wonder who she was," she said.

"I think...it's possible she killed the man. I mean, she was in the same area."

"Maybe. She could have also been a friend. A family member. A lover. Who knows?"

"I don't think so. It's just a feeling I have."

"So, why *didn't* you say anything?"

Nothing in her tone was accusatory. But still, I felt defensive.

"I don't know. She was young, maybe a little older than us. But she wasn't one of us. She was a Wastelander for sure."

Khloe was quiet. It made me nervous since she was always chatty.

"You can't tell anyone," I said. "I know you won't, but I just want to be sure. Something bad could happen if anyone found out."

"Does your dad know?"

"I told him after dinner. He didn't have the chance to give me advice because Chan walked in."

Khloe winced. "He didn't hear anything, did he?"

"I'm sure he didn't. If he did, I would be talking to him now instead of you."

"I guess that's true."

"I can't tell anyone. I can't." I shook my head. "Maybe she killed him. But something tells me there's more to it than that. And...I didn't want her to die. If I had said something, Michael would have been forced to do something about it." I shrugged. "Maybe he noticed, too, but didn't say anything, either."

"Maybe," Khloe said. "Who knows how many Wastelanders have slipped through the cracks that way? I know we're taught they're dangerous, but they're people, just like us, right? Point is, you shouldn't feel bad. Something inside you told you to stay quiet. As far as you know, that's the right choice. Don't beat yourself up about it."

"Yeah. Maybe you're right."

Then again, maybe not. After all, hadn't that woman been the only one around when the man had been stabbed to death? The woman was a Wastelander, and all Wastelanders have the capacity for violence. Who was to say she wouldn't lead anyone else here?

Would I be the reason for the fall of Bunker 108?

"You can't keep thinking like that," Khloe said. "You got to believe that you did right, or you'll go crazy."

I nodded. Anyone could have explained it to me using those words, but because it was Khloe, they stuck.

"Thanks," I said. "You are right."

Khloe smiled. "Of course I am. Girls are *always* right."

"I guess so."

"What happened to the guy you brought in?"

"He's in quarantine."

"Quarantine? Is he sick?"

"He's sick with the xenovirus. Not directly, but there are infected microbes in his bloodstream that are killing him. My dad thinks he doesn't have long, now."

Even in the darkness, I could see Khloe's face go white.

"The xenovirus isn't supposed to affect people. Is it?"

"No. Like I said, it's not affecting him directly. It's getting him sick through the microbes, which are tainted. My dad is hoping to cure him, but I'm not so optimistic. My dad's been working on the xenovirus for a long time."

"Will *you* be alright? You were around him..."

"Well, I'd be lying if I said I wasn't worried. My dad said as long as I didn't touch the wounds, I would be fine. I don't think I touched anything."

"*Think?*"

"I'm pretty sure I didn't."

She sighed. "I don't like that answer."

"I feel fine," I said.

"You need to wash up. You probably didn't even wash your hands before eating."

She smiled, and touched my face. I felt my cheeks redden – I hadn't expected that.

She pulled her hand back. There was dirt on it.

"*Told* you."

Before I had a chance to react, a shadow fell over us from the still ajar door to the corridor.

We both got up, and spun around.

It was Chan.

Chapter 6

Chan stood in the doorway, surveying us with his cold eyes. Khloe and I just stared at him, shocked. After a long while, he spoke.

"Miss Kline, please return to your family's lodgings. I must speak with Alex alone."

Khloe nodded, casting me a worried glance.

"Mr. Keener. Follow me."

I followed Officer Chan, my thoughts racing. What did he know? How could he know anything at all? My dad wouldn't have said anything...would he?

We entered a hallway I rarely frequented – the Officers' Wing. Chan's office was at the end. A guard who I recognized, but whose name I did not know, was posted by the door. He cast me a suspicious glance and said nothing as Chan and I entered.

Chan's office had a desk with a computer and papers on it. On either side was the same, nondescript wooden chair. On the far wall hung a large map, detailing southern California in the Old World. Red pins were stuck in key places, though only Chan and perhaps a few others knew their significance. The office was bare, utilitarian.

"You may sit," Chan said.

I sat in the chair, though Chan remained standing, facing away from me. Though short, he appeared tall and domineering.

"Close the door, Officer Burton."

The officer nodded, and shut the door. The silence that followed was thick.

"How was your first recon, Alex?"

It seemed a strange question, given he knew what happened.

"I wish it could have gone more simply."

Chan wheeled around to face me, hands behind his back. I heard him crack his knuckles. His lips remained horizontal, but I saw him smirk with his eyes.

"I have called you in for two reasons. The first was to inform you that a new strain of the xenovirus has been discovered."

I stared at Chan for a moment in mute shock. It was just thirty minutes ago that I had left the medical bay, believing that it was only the microbes that were infected, and not the man himself.

"What?" I asked.

"I watched as your father ran another test after you left. I personally saw him place the man's DNA under a microscope, and clearly, whatever it showed was *not* entirely human. Your father never thought the xenovirus would be advanced enough to affect a human directly, hence why he would only think to test for the microbes to begin with." Chan smiled grimly. "I'm glad that I insisted your father do this. I had a very bad feeling about this from the beginning."

I was still so overwhelmed with the ramifications of a new strain of the xenovirus, one that affected *humans* no less, I could not answer. If the man were infected, then it could be communicable.

"I wanted to confirm this result to you in person first," Chan said. "Since you help your father with his research, he will naturally share this breakthrough with you. You are *not* permitted, however, to share it with anyone else, under any circumstance. This is the main reason why I brought you here. You must promise me that this will remain hidden until I say otherwise. Do you understand?"

"Yes," I said. "Of course. So, the xenovirus is actually *transforming* the man we found? As it would plants?"

Chan nodded. "Your father is still in the medical bay, working hard to understand this new threat. The man – whoever he is – is beyond saving. We can only watch as his body deteriorates, and take note of the effects the xenovirus has on him. Hopefully, we can learn all we can before he expires."

I remained silent in the pause that followed.

"Now, Alex...did you tell anyone about the man? Perhaps you told Miss Kline?"

I felt a bit frazzled, so it was all I could do to look Chan in the eye. "No. We were talking about school, for the most part. I mentioned that the guy was sick, but nothing more."

Chan nodded. "I hope that was all it was, Alex. Because if this gets out, then there could be one less Bunker in operation by tomorrow."

He said nothing more on that subject, and neither did I.

"Now, I also wanted to know what happened on the recon. Recount everything, beginning to end, and spare no detail. Any piece of information could be important, even if you believe it is trivial. Please, be specific as possible."

"Alright."

I told him. He seemed uninterested in what I said, but I saw his eyes, calculating, when I could bring myself to look at them. When I got to the part of coming upon the man, he became more alert.

"I saw the man, and he had several wounds in his back. I watched Michael as he radioed back for help. We moved him..."

Chan stopped me there. "You saw nothing else? No one else? Obviously this man could not stab *himself* in the back. There had to have been someone else there, no?"

Here, my face twitched. I hoped it escaped Chan's notice. I'm sure it probably didn't.

"No. Just the man."

"It seems strange that a man with stab wounds would be alive like that. It suggests the wounds were rather recent. The person who inflicted the wounds would still be nearby by necessity. You saw nothing – no form, no footprints, no clues, as to whether there had been someone else present?"

"No. If I saw footprints or anything I would have told Michael. I guess he didn't see anything, either."

Chan just stared at me, willing more information out. Finally, he nodded slowly, as if I had just confirmed something he suspected.

"When the Bunkers were first established, there were one hundred and forty four – as you are well aware from your schooling. Now, how many are there?"

"Four."

"Four." He paused, to let it sink in. "You are too young to know this, Alex, being only sixteen. But since that day in 2030, when the Bunkers were filled, there was hope. The Bunkers would arise and rebuild the nation Ragnarok had destroyed. But the Bunkers failed, one by one. Most were wiped out by Wastelanders. The commanders of the Bunkers were lax in security, too generous in charity. They allowed survivors in, gave away food. They didn't keep their locations secret. They could not bring themselves to shoot those who wandered by.

"And some...some Bunkers disappeared into the night – here one day, gone the next, with no rhyme or reason why. The situation has worsened as communication satellites have fallen into disrepair, making contact with any Bunker near impossible."

Chan paused, his eyes narrowing.

"Do you know why we are still alive, Alex? Do you know why we have not fallen, just four of one hundred and forty four Bunkers that still function?"

"Because no one knows we're here."

"That is correct. No one knows we are here. So why go on recons at all? Well, we only send recons out in pairs, except in extreme circumstances, once every week. The senior is taught to look for things the junior is not privy to. Needless to say, it is a very important task, well worth the risk of being discovered. Very few wander near here because they have learned to avoid this area. But the Wasteland is a fluid place – things change, and if we can't keep tabs on our environment, we cannot adapt to ever shifting situations, and may find ourselves eliminated in that way.

"I am Chief Security Officer. It is my job to maintain the security and well-being of all Bunker residents. I am endowed by the government of the United States of America to run this facility, and have been given license to do whatever is necessary to ensure that. Whatever the cost."

He stared at me, a while longer. Almost, he broke me with that will. But at last, he relented.

"If you remember anything about your recon, you can find me personally. Remember what I said about the xenovirus. Not a word." He paused. "That is all."

Just like that, the interrogation was over. Chan turned his attention to some papers, and seemed to have forgotten me in quick order.

But I had to ask one question.

"Officer Chan...why was that man coming to our Bunker, anyway?"

Chan looked up, trying to decipher what I knew. Finally, he spoke.

"It is a matter of governmental security that I cannot relay to you," he said. "That he died in transit was most unfortunate. How he came to be infected in the first place..." Chan frowned, lost in thought. "That is all I have to say on that subject."

"Yes, Officer Chan."

I left Chan to his work, closing the door behind me.

Questions raced through my mind as I walked home. By the time I returned to mine and my father's apartment, it was 21:00. Only then did I allow myself to relax. As soon as I shut the door, I heaved a huge sigh. Chan was the one person whose bad side I didn't want to be on. Up until now, I had done well in not drawing attention to myself. And now, this. Chan would forever remember this, and it might make things difficult.

At least I had my dad to help with things. Tomorrow, after class, I would speak with him. He would know what to do.

I closed my eyes, trying to find peace. When I opened them, I looked at my familiar surroundings. Our apartment was two rooms – a bedroom, and a small living room. The living room contained a couch, several bookshelves filled to overflowing, and a large desk littered with papers and yet more books, where I did my homework and my sketches.

I went to the bedroom, and lay down on the corner bunk. It was a while before I fell asleep. After what Chan told me, it was a wonder I could sleep at all.

I could only hope the morning would bring answers and resolution.

Chapter 7

That morning, I went to class. It was hard to concentrate as Mrs. Watson introduced the class to geometric proofs.

When lunch break came, Khloe walked up to me.

"What happened last night?"

"It was fine. He didn't get anything out of me."

I turned around to leave.

"Wait. Where are you going?"

"I need to go see my dad. He didn't come home last night."

"Is he not sleeping?"

"No. And he probably won't until he's solved this. I'm his voice of reason. That, and I need to figure out what to do about Chan."

"Need company?"

"Sure. I could use the moral support."

We left the classroom, and headed for the medical bay. It wasn't far. We were there within a minute.

It was completely empty. Not even my father's assistants were there.

"Did everyone go home?" Khloe asked.

That's what I thought, at first. Then I realized...

"He must be with the patient."

We walked to the operation room. Through the small window in the door, we could see the patient sprawled on his back, motionless. But that's not what worried me. CSO Chan was standing next to my dad and two assistants. All wore breathing masks.

We ducked out of the way, before any of them could see us.

"What is it?" Khloe whispered.

"Chan's in there," I said.

"Should we leave?"

"No. I want to listen."

"Oh, Alex. Do you really want to get into more trouble?"

"I'm already in trouble. Besides, this is too important."

Khloe sighed. "Fine. I'll stay too, I guess."

I leaned against the door, and listened.

"Will he expire soon?"

It was Chan. I heard whispers from the assistants. Then, my father's voice.

"Yes. He is dead now, in fact. But the virus is changing him. He is no longer human."

"What do you mean?" Chan asked.

"Just that. The DNA is so changed as to no longer be human. All of his hair is gone. The muscles have thickened, and an MRI has shown that there has been a great reduction in brain matter. There are so many changes being made that it is impossible to take note of them all, much less determine their implications. But of note is a strange knot forming in the brain – not a tumor, or cancer, but a great nexus of neural activity in the amygdala and hippocampus that far exceed that of a normal human."

"What does that mean?"

"We have no idea. Those areas of the brain are related to memory and emotion, to put it simply. Why there is growth in both of them and deterioration in other areas, I don't know. It may not even matter. By this point, the patient is dead. His body temperature is the same as this room. No one could survive that."

They were all quiet.

"Well," Chan said. "Perform what tests you need to. Learn all you can. When you're finished, have him incinerated. I will not risk him infecting others."

At that moment, Chan's voice dropped off. I learned closer, thinking they were only speaking more softly.

"Is...is he moving?" one of the assistants asked.

There was a long pause. I stopped breathing. Then, my curiosity won over caution, and I lifted my eyes to the window.

All of them were so transfixed on the body that they were not looking in my direction. The body appeared still, just as it had before.

Khloe stood next to me, also watching through the window. Chan was facing away.

Then, the body jerked, causing all the men to jump back. The legs convulsed, planting themselves on the floor. The eyes opened, two completely white orbs. The arms reached out for one of the assistants.

"Get him away!" he screamed.

Chan pulled out a handgun, pointing it at the patient. "*Freeze!*"

The patient pressed forward, paying no heed. He leaned into the assistant.

Chan fired. The bullet entered the patient's head, splattering the wall and the assistant with purple and grayish goo. The patient collapsed to the ground. The smell was so foul that it permeated the door. I gagged.

Immediately, Chan turned, his eyes burning into me like fire. They narrowed as he scowled, his left cheek twitching. It was the most emotion I'd ever seen out of him, and it terrified me.

He still held the gun in his hand, and he holstered it.

"Clean this mess up," he snapped to the assistants.

My father was now looking at me with his soft, brown eyes, wondering why, of all places, I was here. I felt guilty – doubly, because I knew I had gotten Khloe into trouble, too. I would take the fall for that as well.

But Khloe was not even looking at me. She was still looking at the body with widening eyes. She pointed through the window.

"Oh my God..."

The body on the floor was bloating, fattening, swelling in all the limbs and chest like a balloon.

Everyone stared at the body in horror, now fat and trembling uncontrollably. The skin stretched as liquid beneath it bulged outward. Then, it erupted with a sickening plop. Purple, gray, and red splattered the walls, the ceiling, covering the window through which I watched.

The stench made me vomit in my mouth.

I turned aside to spit it out. Khloe grabbed me by the shoulders, pulling me into the main part of the medical bay.

I didn't merely feel physically sick, but emotionally sick. My dad was in there.

My dad, who was probably now infected with the xenovirus.

Chapter 8

Khloe pulled me away from the door and back into the medical bay. We stood there, unsure of what to do.

"Stay here," Khloe said. "It might be okay..."

No words could describe the horror we had witnessed. The man had come back to life and exploded. I didn't see how it was possible. But there was no denying what I had seen.

The door opened. The four men walked into the medical bay. The purple slime covered their heads, their bodies, their mouths, their eyes. The odds of them escaping the xenovirus now were slim to none.

They stared at us. I could see nothing but horror. My father, having removed his glasses, stared at the floor. Chan, however, was eerily calm. I could see hate in his eyes, as if I were to blame for what had happened.

"Everyone, to the showers," my father said. He looked at me as he said this, though I knew he was not talking to me. "There is still a chance it might not be too late."

There was an air of defeat in his voice.

"Stay here," Chan said to us. "You are not to leave."

They filed off for the showers, leaving Khloe and me alone in the med bay.

"Maybe...maybe they'll be okay..." Khloe said. "It's not impossible, is it?"

"I don't know."

We just stood there, not talking, for the whole time we waited. I could not suppress the sickening dread I felt. Ten minutes later, all four men reemerged wearing scrubs.

Before anyone else could, Chan spoke.

"Stay here," he said. "Stay here, and wait."

Officer Chan raised his communicator.

"Officer Hutton, report to the medical bay, immediately."

Everyone waited in silence for the one minute it took for Officer Hutton to come. When he entered the bay, he stopped short, his normally stony demeanor shocked. He was of average height and a broad build, and had a trim black beard and short, black hair. Burt Hutton was Chan's second in command.

"What is going on?" Officer Hutton asked, eyeing the four men's scrubs up and down.

"Come with me," Chan said. "All of you. Alex, Khloe, Hutton...stay on the other side of Dr. Keener's desk."

We followed Chan into my father's office. He sat down in the chair. For the first time in my life, I saw Chan scared. His face was white.

Khloe, Officer Hutton, and I stood by the door. The other four men stood on the far side of the desk.

The room was quiet for a long while. Then, Chan looked up.

"There is not a small chance," he began, "that me, Dr. Keener, and assistants Ybarra and Jones will soon fall ill and die."

Hutton's eyes widened. "What is this, some sort of joke?"

"Officer Hutton," Chan said, "you know full well that the chance that my words are true far outweighs the chance that I would joke about a matter of such gravity."

Hutton stared at Chan in shock. But Chan went on, regardless.

"In a matter of days – maybe even hours, I will likely be dead, along with everyone else who was in the room with the patient. We are infected with the xenovirus, a strain that targets humans."

I searched my father's eyes for some other answer – any answer that was not this. But he was grave and clearly believed in his own doom as much as Chan.

Chan was giving Hutton instructions on what to do. To assemble the officers, making them aware of the situation. To post a constant guard of four officers by the medical bay, allowing no one to enter or exit. Chan gave Officer Hutton full authority to do all this, and as Chan's second, to assume control of the Bunker.

It sounded so clinical, the way Chan made plans for four eventual deaths. How could his mind work so clearly at a time like this? It made me hate him, the fact he was not even acknowledging the tragedy of the situation.

My dad was dying.

"Lead the children out, and return them to their families."

"This is my family!" I yelled, pointing at my dad. "He is all I have!"

Everyone was looking at me – Khloe and my father, with tears in their eyes.

"It will be alright, son," my dad said. "I'll be fine."

"How do you know that?" I asked, tears stinging my eyes. "You don't."

"You can stay with us," Khloe whispered.

"That will do nicely," Chan said, glad to have me out of the way.

"Dad....is this it? Will I ever see you again?"

He looked at me without a word. This time, he did not lie. His eyes told me everything.

I walked up, meaning to hug him.

"Stop!" Chan yelled. "You are close enough!"

I halted in my tracks.

"Chan," my father said, "that is enough."

"I will not risk any contraction of the disease. That I even allow this is a mercy. The children have both been in here long enough."

I looked at my dad, tears beginning to sting my eyes.

"It'll be alright, son," he said. "You need to do as Officer Chan says. It may yet be alright. I feel fine now."

"Dad..."

"Step away," Chan said. "That is quite enough."

I turned to him, my fists clenched.

"Alex," my father said. "Do not waste words. This is not the end for you. I know you believe it is...but it isn't."

I stared at him through my tears.

"You must be strong, son. There are people depending on you. You are a man. Never forget that. What does a man do?"

I recalled the words he had told me what seems hundreds of times.

"A man does not do what he wants," I said. "He does what he must."

"Yes. Never forget it. I don't want to stay here, Alex. None of us do. I must."

"What will I do without you?"

He looked at me for a long moment, as if he didn't know the answer to that. "It's not over yet, Alex. You must not linger here any longer. You have a duty, to fill your role here. To help people. To protect people. To give them your strength."

Chan nodded to Hutton. Hutton placed a hand on my shoulder. As he guided Khloe and me out of the room, I did not resist him.

"I love you, Alex. Never forget that."

"I love you, too, Dad."

"When you have escorted them out, Officer Hutton, return here," Chan said. "I will brief you on what is to be done next."

Hutton nodded. "Let's go, kids."

Grabbing each of us in his large, meaty hands, he pulled us out of my dad's office and across the bay. I was doing all I could to hold it together, but I knew it wouldn't be long until I burst.

Khloe and I left the medical bay, and Hutton turned back inside, shutting the double doors behind him. Two burly officers in helmets stationed themselves by the door.

I walked across the corridor and sank against the wall.

Then, Khloe's face filled my vision. She placed a hand on my right cheek, wiping my tears away.

"Come on," she whispered. "Let's get you home. He might be alright, Alex. He seemed fine when we were in there."

"I hope so," I said.

But even as I said it, I knew it was a long shot.

She sat down next to me. We sat like that, for a while. People walked by, asking what happened. I didn't answer. Khloe didn't answer. She just held me like I was a child. The guards would quietly explain that the medical bay was off limits, and gave no reason for why. They mentioned nothing about my father, Chan, or my father's assistants.

"They don't know..." I whispered.

Khloe did not answer. Soon, there was such a crowd that I couldn't stand it. I needed to be alone.

I started to get up.

"Come with me," she said, pulling me by the wrist. "You need to rest."

"I need my dad."

She did not argue. Gently, yet firmly, she pulled me with her. I felt a pulsating emptiness in my soul. The only thing connecting me to reality was Khloe.

We reached her family's apartment. I lay down on her bed as she went to the main room to talk to her parents and explain what was going on. While there, I felt completely alone.

Her parents came in, but I don't remember anything they told me. I just closed my eyes, tuning out everything.

When I opened my eyes again, the light was out. I had fallen asleep. I stared for what seemed hours at a picture on the nightstand of Khloe and her family. The picture was old – Khloe was smaller, and her little sister stood next to her, smiling. Abby had been dead now for two years.

Death. So much death. The Wasteland was not out there. It was in here.

Chapter 9

It was night, and the lights were out. Khloe was sleeping on the floor next to me.

I reached down and nudged her.

"What?" she asked, voice thick with sleep.

"I can't let you sleep there."

Khloe wiped her eyes. "Don't be stupid. You need to sleep."

"So do you. There's room for you here."

She stood up. Her face was tender as her eyes gazed into mine.

I was on the verge of tears as I recalled the events of the day. I put my hands to her beautiful face, letting them slide down her neck and rest on her shoulders. She lay down in front of me as I pulled her closer. We stared into each other's eyes.

I closed my eyes and wrapped my arms around her, drawing her close, enjoying her warmth, feeling her heartbeat.

"I feel like you're all I have, now," I said.

Khloe didn't say anything for a while. "I was so sad when I lost my sister. We fought so much, and I lost her. I still feel guilty about it. I wish I didn't have to. I think that's part of being human, though. We wish we could control things, but we can't. It's always too late."

I opened my eyes. Khloe was looking at me.

"Not always," I said.

I leaned forward to kiss her, her lips soft and warm. She kissed me back tenderly, healingly.

She *was* all I had, now. I didn't ever want to let go and feel the emptiness again.

We fell asleep in each other's arms. For one moment, everything was almost okay.

***

I was on the edge of consciousness when the wailing of klaxons shocked me awake. Red light bathed the room. I shot up in bed, Khloe's hand latching onto my arm like a vise.

The siren screamed, over and over, fading in and out.

"What's happening?" Khloe asked.

"I don't know. Where are your parents?"

"They're on nightshift at the lab."

By lab, Khloe meant the hydroponics lab – the largest room in the Bunker. It was located in the subbasement, near the generators. It was where all the food was grown.

I pulled on my hoodie. The siren, coupled with the red light, made me feel like I was living in a surreal nightmare. Maybe I was.

"Let's go into the other room," I said.

We got up and went to the living room. We stood by the intercom. In the event of an alarm, it was what we were supposed to do. But no reassuring voice came. Maybe it would never come.

My father...what if something had happened? What if he had gone haywire, like the man Chan had shot down?

Khloe looked at me, searching my eyes.

"My father is dead," I said. "He is dead."

"How do you know? Maybe..."

"What else could it be? My father, Chan, the others...they got out of the med bay, somehow. And if it's anything like the patient, then we're all in a lot of trouble."

Khloe grabbed my hand. "You're right. We have to go."

"Go where?"

"Out."

"Outside?"

Then, I heard screams. A gunshot. A snarl. A body falling, outside our door to the corridor. I felt coldness creep over me.

Something was out there.

I could not deal with this. Not now.

I looked madly for something that could be used as a weapon. A lamp. A large book.

A skillet in the kitchen.

I ran to get it as the door slammed open. I stared up. It was an officer, hairless, his eyes wild and completely white. For a moment, I froze in my tracks. Two lacerations split his face open, where someone had slashed him with a knife. He stumbled forward, toward Khloe.

Khloe screamed. But instead of cowering as I might have done, she ran toward him, pushing him back outside. The attacker growled, and went for her again.

Skillet in hand, I charged the officer. Khloe screamed again, pushing on the man's shoulders. His mouth snapped viciously toward her neck. She punched him in the face. I clobbered the officer's head with the skillet. He fell to the ground, and I smashed his head in, again and again. His eyelids fluttered, then stilled, revealing completely white orbs. Purplish blood oozed from his mouth.

That's when I noticed his body quivering and bloating.

"Run!"

We ran past the man and into the corridor. I slammed the door shut. Just in time, because I heard a sickening pop. As I held the door closed, I felt it vibrate as it was splattered with goo from the other side.

We paused for a moment to collect our breaths.

"What is going on?" Khloe asked.

I looked down, noticing the officer had dropped a handgun by the door. I grabbed it, checking the magazine for bullets. There were four left.

"Like you said. We're leaving."

"What about my parents? We need to get to the hydroponics lab."

"We've got to go there now," I said. "Take this. You might need it."

I handed Khloe the skillet. She took it with wide eyes.

She led the way. I followed her through the empty hall, my gun at the ready. The wailing sirens and lights bathed the floor in eerie red.

We turned the corner and found a body, already ruptured. Purple goop dripped from the ceiling. A line of slime fell, missing my face by a hair.

"Watch the ceiling," I said. "Any of that stuff gets inside of you, you're done."

Khloe nodded, shaky.

We entered the commons. The room was empty, but I heard voices and the sounds of a struggle coming from a hallway leading from the other side. Several dead bodies lay on the floor, mutilated. I recognized the corpse of one of my classmates, Vincent Corley. He had been athletic, smart, and popular.

Now, his right arm was completely ripped off.

"Vincent..." Khloe said.

Then, gunshots sounded in the distance, followed by bloodcurdling screams and inhuman wails. They were coming from the direction of the caf.

"We can't go that way," I said.

"There are stairs nearby," Khloe said. "Follow me."

We went down two flights, to the lowest level in the Bunker. After the first flight, we heard someone's raspy breath just a few feet away. I did not know if they were one of the infected, or just injured. Either way, we didn't stay to find out. We quietly descended the second flight without his or her knowing.

We were now in front of the door that led into the hydroponics lab. We entered, finding ourselves among aisles and aisles of plants bearing enough fruits and vegetables to sustain several hundred people year-round. Unlike the rest of the Bunker, this room, if it could be so called because it was so enormous, smelled fresh. All the aisles added together were miles long.

I enjoyed coming here from time to time, but now, the place was dark and frightening. I did not know what horrors could be hiding in the shadows, around the next corner.

"Mom? Dad?" Khloe called.

Khloe's voice echoed and died.

We walked the aisles, one by one, checking each. But the entire room seemed empty.

"We should have stayed home," Khloe said. "They probably went back to get us..."

"Maybe."

"I can't leave without them," Khloe said. "It wouldn't be right."

Just then, a door slammed open. I spun on my heels, raising my gun. When I saw it was Khloe's parents, I lowered my weapon.

"Mom! Dad!"

Khloe ran and threw herself on her mom. Mr. and Mrs. Kline embraced her, racked with sobs.

"Thank God you're here," Mrs. Kline said.

Mr. Kline said nothing – he only held his daughter as if he never wanted to let her go.

Both had brown hair. Mr. Kline had a bookish look to him, and wore black-rimmed glasses. Despite this, he was tall and fit. Mrs. Kline was short, a little stout, but in shape. She had kind, gentle eyes.

I felt an intense sense of relief at seeing them. However, the reunion was dragging on too long.

"We need to leave," I said.

"Yes," Mr. Kline said. "We just came from the caf. There are about a dozen making a stand. The rest..."

"We have more of chance out there than in here," I said.

"You're right," Mr. Kline said. "There's an exit that leads to the atrium this way. Follow me."

We followed Mr. Kline to a corner of the lab. There was a small, nondescript door, locked by a keycard. Mr. Kline used his card. It beeped, and the lock clicked open.

"Only your mother and I, and some of the officers have access to this area," Mr. Kline said. "It's where we recycle the hydroponic fluid."

We passed rows of blue barrels, all filled with the nutrient-rich liquid needed to grow the plants in the next room without soil. The room itself was massive, filled with large, complex machinery. Mr. Kline was the operator of the recycling tanks, and probably the only person who knew the intricacies of the machines. Thick hoses left the room through the wall in order to feed the huge farms of the lab. This room was, arguably, the most important in the entire Bunker. Without it, everyone starved. No wonder it was kept so secure.

We walked through the room, until we reached the opposite side. There, we entered a thin, claustrophobic hallway that was little-used. At the end was a circular stairway, leading up. Mr. Kline went first, followed by Khloe, then her mom. I went last.

Mr. Kline opened the door at the top. When I stepped through it, we found ourselves in the atrium of Bunker 108. The exit was one minute away.

"We made it," I said.

The circular vault door leading into the exit tunnel was wide open. Some had already escaped.

"Keep your gun ready," Mr. Kline said.

I held my gun up as we advanced.

We entered, finding the rocky exit tunnel dimly lit. The temperature was near freezing. Between us and the final vault door, were two forms: one on the ground, bloody and dead, and the other kneeling beside it.

Before anyone could speak, the man's face snapped toward us.

It was Chan, his all-white eyes empty and soulless. Wet, red blood stained his uniform. His head cocked to the right side. All his muscles tensed.

He charged forward, letting out an otherworldly bellow.

"Get back!" Mr. Kline yelled.

I aimed my gun and fired three times. The bullets entered Chan's body – his chest, his abdomen, his right arm. From each wound, purple goo shot out, like it had replaced the blood in his body.

None of the shots had any effect. Chan only stumbled on, set on one goal – killing us at any cost.

I had one shot left. I aimed for the head, watching it bob up and down as Mr. Kline pulled away from Chan.

I fired.

I missed probably by inches.

Khloe screamed as Chan tackled her father to the ground. I dropped my gun and ran to pull Chan off him.

But it was too late. Mr. Kline screamed as Chan ripped into his neck, tearing from it a tendril of bloody flesh. Mr. Kline's horrible howl became choked with blood. A small fountain of blood shot upward.

Khloe ran up from behind, letting out a desperate scream. She smashed Chan's head in with the skillet, bludgeoning him until his animalistic eyes rolled back. He keeled over and collapsed on the ground.

Almost instantly, Chan's body started to inflate.

"Run!" Khloe screamed.

I pulled Khloe back, away from the swelling body. I could see Khloe's mom and dad were beyond all hope of escaping the blast. Khloe and I ducked behind a corner just as Chan exploded. A wall of purple slime gushed past us.

We reemerged to find both of Khloe's parents coated with the stuff.

"No," Khloe said. "No..."

She ran forward.

"No!" her mother yelled. "Do not touch me! You have to go." Tears ran down Mrs. Kline's face, cutting a clear path through the slime.

Mr. Kline lay on the ground, twitching, choking. It looked like he was trying to speak, but to no avail.

Khloe's face was white as she stared at her dying father.

"I..." she said.

"You can't stay here," Mrs. Kline said. "Go!"

Khloe recoiled as if struck.

"Go, Khloe," Mrs. Kline said, desperately. "Run now. You will not die here."

"Khloe," I said. "We have to go."

Behind us, I could hear gunshots, people screaming, and non-human growling. I looked toward the vault door.

"*Come on*, Khloe!"

More snarls, and the pattering of footsteps from the atrium.

"Goodbye," she said. "I love you..."

I pulled her toward the exit, just as she had pulled me along when my father was dying. Though I had no strength, I had to be strong.

I had to do what I must, not what I wanted.

We ran down the corridor, and did not look back. People who had been alive and well only hours earlier now flooded the tunnel. I had no idea how, but the xenovirus was turning humans into crazed monsters. They charged forward, their hellish white eyes paralyzing me with fear.

Together, Khloe and I turned the wheel on the door. We pushed it open into the cold, pitch black night and howling, shocking wind. We stepped forward, as if into another dimension. Together, we slammed it shut, shutting out Bunker 108 and its infected denizens forever.

The dusty wind blustered, chilling me to the bone. I latched onto Khloe in the darkness. A single tear coursed down her cheek.

We shivered at the wind, and the cruelty of the world.

It felt like the apocalypse happening all over again.

Chapter 10

We stumbled over rocks into the cold, windy darkness. The wind cut like a knife. Our clothes were not sufficient protection against it. We had no light. We could only hope, by some miracle, that we came across some form of shelter for the night.

After a few minutes, I looked back, and could see nothing but black night, feel nothing but the wind and sand stinging my face, could hear nothing but the maelstrom and Khloe, crying next to me.

"Just a little farther," I said.

Even though she was with me, I still felt alone, because the wind ate my words as black holes eat light.

Then, we ran right into something hard and metallic. I felt along the surface, and wanted to cry for joy.

"The trailer," I said. "We have to find the door."

For minutes we searched, until I found the latch that led inside. I pushed Khloe in, and slammed the door against the merciless cold.

I found the light, and flipped it on. It was mostly bare. A small kitchen sat in front of us, and beyond that, a worn couch. I could see the door to the bathroom. The light could barely reach it, but at the end, I could make out the corner of a bed.

Khloe went to the couch, and crashed down, and began sobbing all over again.

There was a red, fleece blanket on the couch. I took it and wrapped it around her.

I sat next to her for a minute, shivering. Without a word, she took the blanket and wrapped it around both of us.

We let ourselves thaw for a minute. Then, I got up and went to fridge. Inside was a container filled with ice. I tried to turn on the stove to heat the trailer up. It didn't work.

I locked the front door, and made sure the shutters were drawn shut. I went back to the fridge to get the container of ice. I had to find a way to heat it, but could see nothing I could do – nothing until morning came. Its warmer temperatures could get us something to drink by noon.

A quick glance in the cabinet revealed a few homemade granola bars. My stomach growled. I grabbed four of them and headed back to the couch.

Khloe was lying down now, a hand over her face. I sat next to her.

"Here," I said, "I found some granola."

She was still shaking.

"I feel sick," she said.

"You're just cold," I said. "Close your eyes."

"That makes it worse."

"Then look at me."

Her eyes fluttered open, slowly. They were red, and her face was so pale and blue. Even her lips were blue.

"Here," I said. "Eat some of this."

"I feel sick."

"Lay down," I whispered. "You'll be alright."

I lay with my front against her back. Every part of her was cold. I started eating, even if she couldn't. I needed all the warmth I could get. I rubbed her back, her arms, her fingers, trying to create some blood flow.

I got up to get the container of ice. I returned to the couch and put it under with us so that it might melt. I kissed her face, her ears. They felt like ice on my lips. Finally, she stopped shivering, and I heard her even breaths. She was asleep.

I stayed like that, trying not to let myself fall asleep in case anything else happened.

***

I had fallen asleep sometime in the night, despite my commitment to staying up. Khloe was still asleep, her breaths slow. Too slow. Her heart beat so faintly.

"Khloe?"

I shook her gently. Her skin was clammy, burning up. I felt her forehead. She was on fire.

"No..." she rasped. "No..."

I got up, and knelt on the floor, looking into her face. Her eyes flickered open. They were just as red, and so dim I was not sure she even saw or understood I was there.

"Khloe?"

Her eyes had shut, and she opened them again. I opened the shutters, so that at least some of the reddish morning light could filter inside. Her skin was pale, dry, and hot. She fought for every breath.

"Khloe!"

Her eyes shot open. "What? Where am I? What is this?"

I reached for the water. Over half of it had melted in the night. Though my throat was parched and screamed to be satisfied, I held the water to Khloe's lips

"Drink this, okay?"

Her lips moved weakly along the rim of the container. I tilted it, ever so slightly. The liquid entered her mouth. She tried to swallow, but coughed it up.

"It's okay," I said.

I grabbed her shoulders, softly pulling her up. I realized then just how frail she was, how the night and the cold had taken its toll on her body.

"Drink some water. Just one swallow. That's it."

She gave a weak nod. I held the container to her lips once more. This time, she drank several gulps.

"There you go," I said.

Her eyes opened. "Is there any for you?"

"I already had mine," I said. "Here. Eat something."

I took some granola, breaking it up into small pieces. She grabbed one of the pieces from me with her right hand. I noticed a mark on her wrist.

Teeth marks.

I felt my heart stop. She looked in me, her eyes watering. The granola was forgotten, and there was only us, staring into each other's eyes, understanding everything without saying a word.

"I'm sorry," she said.

I cupped her face that burned against my hands like a sun. It was all she could to keep her eyes open and focused on me. I felt my heart ripping apart.

"It happened in the apartment..."

My eyes filled with tears. I couldn't believe this was happening.

"I love you, Alex. I'm...sorry. I was hoping I would be okay. It was such a small thing."

"You did nothing wrong," I said, pulling her close. "I love you, Khloe."

"I...don't want you to think it's your fault..."

"It's not," I said, the tears streaming down my face. "It's not."

I felt so empty now. The world was taking everything from me that mattered. Khloe was all I had left.

I just wondered when my turn would come.

"I won't leave you," I said. "I won't."

"You'll have to," she said. "Maybe...maybe you'll find another home. Another Bunker."

"You are my home."

I stroked her hair, gave her more water as it melted. The trailer heated up as the day progressed. I tried to feed her, but she refused. From time to time, she would cough, and I would wipe whatever phlegm accumulated on her mouth. I would stroke her hair, once so lush and soft, now so dry and wispy. Her once beautiful skin was now sickly, lifeless, pale, translucent, revealing blackened veins. Her face became gaunter as the day progressed.

Soon, she began to stink. But I did not remove myself from her side.

"I love you," I said.

I told her the same thing again and again throughout the day. Her eyes were closed, and I feared they would never open again.

"I..." she said.

Her chest fell, her head slumped, and she leaned against the couch. Every muscle went slack, and some spirit lifted from her face, leaving behind only a body. Her eyes relaxed, and remained half-opened. I stared into her, seeing only a body that looked like Khloe that was not her.

I could not even cry. I stayed, holding her cold hand that grew ever colder which each passing minute. I wanted to be sure she was not really dead.

Her body, by some small, cruel mercy, did not attack me, and did not swell like the others. I didn't know why, and didn't really question it. Maybe since it was a small bite, it would have taken more time.

I kissed her face, so cold and frail. When my lips touched her skin, I thought it would disintegrate.

I went outside in a daze. I found a shed behind the trailer. Inside was a shovel.

I knew what came next. I lost myself in digging a grave not worthy of Khloe. Putting a body in the ground was foreign to me. Everyone in Bunker 108 was cremated.

As I emptied the hole, I emptied myself. Though it was cold, I was covered in sweat by the time I finished.

I laid her body in, and let my tears fall into the grave. I was completely bereft of all hope and life. Khloe had been that for me.

It was an hour before I could bring myself to cover her. I could only think of all the memories Khloe and I had shared.

And now, all hope was gone. She was gone, to be buried in the cold, hard earth, never to move, laugh, or breathe again.

When the last of the grave had been covered, I felt so guilty. I knew objectively that it wasn't my fault. But that did not help. Everyone around me had died. While I longed for death myself, it never visited me.

I could have brought myself to take my own life, but I didn't for one reason – Khloe would not have wanted it, and neither would my father.

I knew them well enough to know that.

***

By the next day, I couldn't stay in the trailer any longer. I had to find somewhere else. Food and water were running low. It was late September, which meant it would be getting cold, soon – too cold to stay anywhere above ground.

I found a backpack in the trailer. I put the container of water inside, as well as the rest of the granola – twenty four bars total. I could eat three a day, which gave me rations for eight days. Eight days to find a new home, or more food – though my caloric intake would be pitiful. I also packed some blankets. I could not count on finding shelter, and needed enough to shield me from the nighttime cold.

Finally, on the morning of the third day after arriving at the trailer, I set off, kissing the loose earth atop Khloe's grave. I marked it, with rocks arranged in the shape of a heart.

I headed toward the sun, rising in the east.

Chapter 11

I knew of several settlements not far from 108 – Oasis, Last Town, and even L.A.. But L.A. was consumed with gang violence, so it wasn't an option.

My goal was to find one of the smaller settlements and try to get taken in. The only problem was, I had no idea where any were.

The morning warmed quickly, but it must have never gotten above fifty degrees. The wind was calm, which I was thankful for. It would be October soon, and I would need warmer clothes.

I didn't have much to my name: my pack, filled with granola and water; my blanket, rolled up and tied with some nylon rope, and the clothes on my back. I didn't even have a weapon. I had forgotten the handgun back in the tunnel – it had been out of ammo, anyway, but it still could have come in handy.

I left behind the line of red mountains where Bunker 108 was hidden. I crested a hill and turned back to see the metal trailer, glimmering in the red midmorning haze. I could see a small spot of turned earth, where Khloe lay. I looked out, north and east, surveying several ramshackle buildings spread over the vast tract of desert and dunes, long conquered by the victorious elements. A crumbled highway, half buried in sand, cut through the twisted landscape, maybe two klicks out. The red sky spread upward like something out of a nightmare. The day was relatively clear, yet still, the meteor fallout reduced the sun to a slightly brighter shimmer on a small part of the sky.

Nothing moved or breathed, save myself.

I walked on. I did not speak a word. In fact, I felt like I would never have reason to speak again.

I don't remember that first week well. All the days blended and I cared for nothing, not even myself. I could only mourn my past life and everything I'd lost, and wonder if there was any point to going on.

At nights, I would hole up in some building that offered the least bit of protection. I would eat my stale granola, drink my water, and curl up in a corner with my blanket and shiver myself to sleep. I cried the first two nights. I had nightmares of Khloe rising from the grave.

I felt hungry and thirsty constantly. When I came across pools of water I would drink from them and refill my container. It was not cold enough to freeze except in the dead of night. I had expected to find food in the buildings. But every cabinet was bare. The Wastelanders had had thirty years to take everything.

I came across ruins often. But I had yet to come across any city, lived in or not.

On the third day, I arrived at a deep gully spanned by a collapsed bridge. I almost fell to my death while picking my path across it.

The Mojave Desert, even in the Old World, had been a dry, harsh place – scant of vegetation and hostile to life. Now, it was even more so. I did not see a single living thing other than the odd bush or barest wisps of grass. Red dunes slanted against the skeleton remains of civilization.

The mountains to the south were almost out of sight, now. They had once been my home.

There were mountains everywhere in the distance - to the south, to the east, to the west. Some areas I walked were flat and bare - others were hilly and mangled. I had no idea where I was going, so I followed the path of least resistance, which often meant following the old roads. In places, the asphalt and concrete still showed.

It was startling how much could be buried and lost in thirty years.

Often, when I camped for the night in a building, I would see a black spot on the floor from previous campfires. I would try to find another place in those cases.

It was a week after I had set out when I came across my first Wastelanders. I was camping in a small hole on the side of a bare, rocky hill, when I heard the laughter. At first, I thought it was my imagination and loneliness. Curiosity made me follow the sound.

As the voices grew louder, I noticed the smell of smoke borne by the wind. Mingled within was a savory aroma that made my stomach growl.

I climbed up the top of a rise, and laid low. Below, in a small depression, six people surrounded a low fire. A giant pot simmered over the flames. My heart raced.

There were five men and one woman, all dressed in dingy military apparel. They were too far to see clearly. All had weapons, mostly rifles, but the woman was armed with a pistol.

Any thought of approaching them was dashed from my mind. Their faces were so hardened they looked more like monsters than humans.

I guessed that these were raiders, the worst kind of Wastelanders, who robbed, stole, and murdered for a living. If I went up to them, they would kill me, or at best take me prisoner.

I would have snuck away, but for one reason: I was low on food, and I needed something to eat. If I waited for them to fall asleep, I could sneak into their camp and take some supplies.

It was desperate, but I saw no other choice. I hadn't found any supplies in my few days out in the Wastes. It was death either way.

For now, they were eating. Each ladled stew into their bowls. While they ate, there was joking and laughing. But somewhere, the conversation took a turn for the worse. The raiders started arguing. One man threw his bowl on the ground in anger. Seeing that stew spill was torture.

The argument seemed to be about the woman. She had stopped looking bored and started looking attentive.

Then, a brawl started between two of the men. One of them raised a gun.

Another gun went off, shattering the silent night. A man with a blonde crew cut had shot dead the man who had drawn the gun.

The man who was shot fell to his knees, then to the ground. Blood pooled by the light of the fire. The man twitched, and everyone watched. Then, he was still.

The three remaining men started stripping the dead man's body of clothing, jewelry, and useful things he had been carrying. The blonde man took the dead man's rifle. No one argued. He was probably in charge.

The dead man, with only his clothes left, was hauled into the night by the men. The woman sat by the fire, watching. The men tossed their fallen comrade into the darkness like unwanted garbage.

After that, everyone was quiet. The blonde man walked to the woman, and whispered something. She turned her face away. He left her to go back to his spot.

Everyone curled up for sleep.

I waited for at least an hour. When they all seemed good and asleep, I decided that now was my chance. I crept forward, toward the fire.

As I neared, I knew I would now be clearly visible to them. Just one look, and I was dead.

But if I did not eat, I was equally dead. I needed food and I needed a weapon.

I did not dare take any food from the pot, however much I wanted to. That risked too much noise.

All were sleeping, their backs to the flame. So far, so good.

I decided to find something immediately and take it away. Any of them could wake up at any moment.

My eyes set upon a hefty backpack sitting next to the man with the blonde crew cut. I nearly jumped out of my skin when he rolled over to face me. Thankfully, his eyes stayed shut. His face had a long, deep scar, running diagonally from the top of his right eye to the left corner of his mouth, right across his pockmarked nose.

After a moment, I reached for the pack. I lifted it slowly, so it would not disturb the stones beneath it. But two of the stones clacked ever so slightly against each other. I winced. The sound must have been a lot louder in my head than in reality. Nothing happened.

The pack was very heavy. My heart raced. There would be lots of supplies in it.

I backed away from the flame, toward the cold night once more. I was going to make it, at least for the next few days.

I was now far enough from the fire to walk normally. I scurried up the slope. I needed to make it to my cave and grab the rest of my stuff. Then, I would set out that night. I needed as much distance between myself and the raiders as possible.

That's when I felt cold hands wrap around my neck.

I couldn't even scream. My head swam as darkness took hold. I fell to the hard earth.

Chapter 12

When I awoke, my head throbbed. Footsteps crunched on the ground near my head.

"Wake up," a female voice said.

I rolled on my back, facing upward. My vision was hazy, and the cave dark, so I could not make out what she looked like. It appeared that she was alone, however.

"Who are you?" I asked. "Was it you who attacked me?"

"*I'm* the one asking the questions, thief."

"Thief?"

"You stole the backpack of one of my friends back there."

"Stole..."

I felt like an idiot. I was just repeating her words. It was like I had forgotten how to speak.

"Are you going to kill me?"

"No," she said. "Lucky for you, I'm ready to split from them. If it had been anyone else who had caught you, you'd be dead."

The woman knelt down. As my vision cleared, and her face got closer, I recognized her instantly. She was the woman who had been watching from behind the rock.

"*You*..." I said, through gritted teeth.

Her eyes went wide with recognition. "You're...you're that Bunker kid. What the hell are you doing out here?"

I stood, clenching my fists. "Everyone I know is dead because of you!"

She stared. "What are you talking about, kid?"

She wasn't that much older than me – maybe nineteen or twenty. She had long, black hair, and hazel eyes. Her skin was a creamy mocha color, and she was well-formed and in shape. She was very pretty. It was hard to place her ethnicity, but she seemed Asian.

"You stabbed that man, and we brought him back," I said. "He infected everyone in the Bunker, and now everyone I know is dead. I should have shot you the minute I saw you!"

I was screaming at her. Why *hadn't* I killed her? Why didn't I tell Michael on the recon? None of this would have happened. My dad, Khloe, everyone else...they would all still be alive.

"Hey, kid. Calm down. I don't want to hurt you."

"*Hurt* me? I don't care what you do to me. I couldn't care less. I have *nothing* now because of you."

"Shut the hell up, and give me a chance to explain myself."

Sizing her up, I knew she could probably take me in a fight. Let's face it; she was a lot more in shape than me, *and* she had a pistol holstered at her side.

I sat down on a large rock.

"Alright," the woman said. "We found the guy lying on the side of the road. He looked dead. We were going to pass him up, but he groaned as we walked past him. We stopped. The guys wanted to kill him. There was nothing I could do to stop them. Brux stabbed him, three times in the back. We hauled his body off the road, where no one would find him.

"Then you guys came, so I hid. I thought you might have seen me. But I guessed you didn't, because you didn't do anything."

"And I should have."

"I had no idea you would take him in. Besides the purple stuff coming out of him, we didn't think he was sick." She blinked. "So, did everyone really die?"

"Yes. Everyone except me. I'm the only one who made it out. At least, the only one I know of. I lost my dad and my friend, among other people."

She looked at me, her eyes wide. "I'm sorry. I really am. But it was a mistake on our part. You have to believe that."

"It doesn't matter. What's done is done. I'm trying to find a city. I won't survive long out here. I was just trying to find some food, which is why I snuck into your camp."

The girl looked me up and down, seeming to see me in a new light. I looked past her, toward the mouth of the cave.

"You're going to die, you know," she said. "They'll come after you. They'll make you wish you were dead."

"I wish I were dead now."

"Don't say that. You keep saying that, and you really *will* be dead. Trust me, you don't really want that."

"What do you know? Maybe I do. My dad is dead, because of you. My friend is dead, because of you. There's nothing you can do to make up for that."

The girl looked at me, and scowled.

"You don't want my help? Fine. But if you decide you want to survive out here, I can teach you everything you need to know. How to make a fire. Where to find food and water. All the good places to camp. Who to trust, who to avoid, what cities will let you in. It will take you years to figure that out on your own. I can teach you in hours."

"Thanks, but I'll be fine on my own."

"I doubt that. How long have you been out here?"

"One week."

"Have you found any food or supplies in that time?"

"No."

"There's only a few kinds of people who would sneak into a raider camp and steal their gear: the insane, the stupid, and the desperate. I think you might be the third, but the first two are sounding pretty good, too."

She handed me the backpack I had stolen. I held it awkwardly in my hands.

"Now, you can either come with me and keep all that stuff, or you can go out on your own without it. Your choice."

I looked up at her. She was serious.

I set the pack on the ground, and rifled through its contents.

"Let me at least see what I would be losing out on."

A pot. Some cans of food. Some bullets.

There was a heavy shirt. Might make a good extra layer for colder nights.

I lifted up the shirt. Below it at the bottom of the pack were dozens upon dozens of small, silver batteries.

"What the hell...?"

"All our pay was in Brux's pack. I'm willing to split it with you, if we work together."

"Batteries? Seriously?"

"They're currency."

"But they're worthless..."

"To you, maybe. With these things, you can walk into just about any settlement and get food, weapons, whatever you want. There's well over three hundred batts in there."

"That's...insane."

"Look, kid. Batts are valuable. They're from the Old World, and they're useful. They give heat, cook food, and power machines that would otherwise be useless. They're a commodity, and someday, all of them will be gone. These are even the cheap kind. If you could get your hands on some rechargeables or solars, you'd never have to raid again."

"Fine, I believe you. So, why would you want to split them with me?"

"Because, believe it or not, I actually feel bad for what happened. Most raiders aren't bad people. We were just in a bad situation, and we do what we must to survive. If I've already 'killed' everyone who matters to you, then maybe this is some weird way to make it up."

"No. There's nothing you can do, so don't even try."

I didn't want to talk to her, and I wanted her to stop talking to me. Yet, she did have a point. I knew nothing about surviving out here. Going with her would give me something to do, even if I hated her guts. Hate was better than emptiness. It would give me a reason to go on.

"Fine," I said. "I'll go with you. Where are we going?"

"Don't know. Somewhere far away from them. Maybe Oasis. It's a walled settlement, so if I can get you in there, you'd be safe. It's run by a man named Ohlan, who I've met. You might be able to buy your citizenship there with your share of the batts."

"Do we have enough food?"

"Just what we have in the pack. You have a name?"

I eyed her up and down. I guess if I was stuck with her for the next few days, names might be useful.

"...Alex Keener."

"Makara Angel."

She lifted her own pack, putting it on her shoulders.

"Come on. If we're fast enough, I know a place where we can shelter before sundown. Keep an eye out. I can't look everywhere at once, and raiders can be thick in this area. It's cold today, so most of the rats will be hiding in their holes. That's good for us. If we hurry, we might make Oasis tomorrow."

Makara headed for the mouth of the cave. The raiders would probably be very close by.

I followed her outside.

Chapter 13

By the time we got going, I realized I was hurting more than I thought. Everything ached, especially my stomach, which hadn't had food in a while. There was little water, too. Makara gave me some of her share. I accepted, even if I didn't want to. As we walked, I munched on some of my granola, fighting back the urge to down all of them.

Makara was always busy scanning the horizon, ducking at random moments. I had no idea what she was so afraid of. We were clearly the only ones out here on this cold, dismal day.

The clouds were spooky looking – always the color of blood, that cast the whole bare earth in crimson light.

"What kind of name is Makara, anyway?"

"It's Khmer. It's the first month of the Cambodian year. I'd like to think it means a new beginning."

Despite myself, I became interested. "Are you Khmer?"

"On my father's side. My mother was American, and so am I, for that matter."

"How are you American? You're a Wastelander."

"I was born here, kid. That makes me American."

***

We stopped around noon to eat. She handed me some sort of sticky, bread-like substance wrapped in tin foil. It wasn't bad.

"What's in this, anyway?" I asked.

"Rice, mostly."

"It tastes good."

Makara smirked. "Hunger is the best seasoning. I'd rather have a hearty stew on a day like this."

We were up again, and walking. We were in the wilderness, nowhere near a city. Makara had taken us far off road, thinking that if we were being followed, it would be harder for her former raid group to track us. Flat plains spread before us. There was a nightmarish beauty to it.

"So, are we anywhere close to L.A.?"

"L.A. is about eighty miles west. Fights, and wars all the time, gangs killing each other over the last bits of stale food that haven't been snatched up. Not much can survive thirty years. Eventually, L.A. will be completely dead. Not like it was ten years ago, when Raine was alive."

"Who was Raine?"

She didn't answer, but kept walking. I shrugged, and didn't ask again.

Nothing more happened that day. No more words were exchanged. I could tell Makara wanted to be alone with her thoughts. Fine by me – so did I.

***

We walked the rest of the day without much incident. When the red sky darkened, Makara led us into an old house, decrepit and peeling. Otherwise, it looked like it had weathered the horrors of Ragnarok pretty well. Its structure was intact, and it didn't look like it would be collapsing anytime soon.

We went inside. We ate the last of my granola bars. From Makara's face, she disliked this even more than the rice bread.

After eating, she got up.

"I need to check something out," she said.

I shrugged. I got out my blanket and hunkered down in a corner. Just to think two weeks ago, I would be in my warm bed full of hopes and dreams. All of that was gone, now.

The numbness just grew until I burst. I tried to hold back tears, but they came out all the same. I kept thinking of Khloe. When one has no hope, one can't even cry. But now, I guessed I had hope.

Hope in what?

Makara came back in. I hastily dried my tears.

"We're not being followed...at least from what I can tell..." She stopped short. "What's wrong?"

I didn't answer her. I couldn't find the words.

"I know things are tough," she said, in her tough voice. "But you need to buck up."

How she could even say that, I didn't know. She had no idea. No idea at all.

I turned toward her. I could see her silhouette by the door.

"You know," Makara said, "you probably won't believe me, but we're a lot alike. That's part of the reason why I wanted you to come with me. I don't fit in with the raider types and I don't fit in with the settler types. If I can get away from the raiding life, I'm willing to risk it."

"You're alone, then."

"Does that surprise you?"

"No. But it makes me wonder what you see in me."

"I see me in you."

I was about to think she truly was crazy, when she surprised me.

"Like you," she said, "I was born in a Bunker."

***

I just stared at Makara. I didn't know what to say.

"Wait... really? Which one?"

"Mine...was a bit different. I was in the main government Bunker. The one with President Garland in it. Bunker One."

Nothing in her voice told me that she was lying. There was nothing I could do to hide my shock.

"Wait...*the* Bunker One? The Bunker one thousand miles away in Cheyenne Mountain, Colorado? What happened to it? How did you end up here?"

"That's a long story."

"Well, we have time."

"I suppose so," Makara said, "though I don't really like to talk about it. Where I'm from, it's much colder, and darker. They call it sunny California for a reason, huh?"

"Doesn't seem too sunny to me."

Makara smiled. "You're hard to please, then."

"What happened to Bunker One? How did it fall?"

"Bunker One was huge. It held ten thousand people."

"Ten...*thousand*...?" I asked. "How did you feed them all? Where did they fit?"

"The Bunker came from the Cold War era. During the Dark Decade, they expanded it. But none of that matters now, because everyone who lived there is dead. Everyone except me, as far as I know."

There was nothing I could say to that. Nothing at all, other than...

"That's what happened to us. People started getting sick, and dying and...turning on each other."

Makara nodded. I was surprised to see none of this surprised her.

"Did Bunker One fall in the same way?" I asked.

"It fell in a similar way. It was an attack of demons."

"Demons?"

"They are what they sound like. They're monsters, from Ragnarok. They're still very rare around here. You can find them in areas called Blights. You'll know them as soon as you see them, because this weird, purple fungus grows thick on the ground and stinks up the land. All the trees are coated with purple slime. All animals avoid it – except the demon animals, and you will know them because they stink like rotting corpses and have all white eyes."

When she said "white eyes," I couldn't help but think of Chan, and everyone the xenovirus infected in Bunker 108. It was an image I had been trying to push out of my mind all week. But it sounded like it had happened at Bunker One, too. Only, that would have been twelve years ago. If that was the case, then the human strain of the xenovirus was much older than my father had thought.

I remained quiet as Makara continued.

"The monsters attack any living thing on sight," Makara said. "That's how unaffected animals turn – they are bitten, and they become part of the Blight."

"So, you're telling me these monsters attacked Bunker One?"

"Yes. They're a lot thicker in Colorado, I guess because it's closer to Ragnarok Crater. But now, it's spreading, even as far as here. It's starting to affect everything. I saw my first Blight in this area about a year ago, farther north. There's more of them, now. There have been mysterious deaths, even by Wasteland standards."

"It's nothing demonic," I said. "It's the xenovirus. I had no idea it was this dangerous. Not until last week, anyway."

"When you live underground, you're blind to what's going on upside. These Blights have been old news here for at least a year."

"What happens to the animals it affects?"

"They become stronger, faster, and deadlier. A huge of wave hit us, that night. Where they all came from, I don't know. There were thousands. But they were animals of all kinds – birds, wolves, even bears – all rotting and twisted, attacking as if of one mind to destroy us. And there were some that have no name, which look like nothing this world has ever seen."

"Were there people turned into them, too?"

"No. I have never seen people turn into these monsters. Is that what happened at your Bunker?"

I nodded. "Yeah. There's apparently a new strain that targets humans, too."

"Then this is only getting worse," Makara said.

"The bodies exploded, sending purple slime everywhere," I said. "That seems to be how it spreads." I thought of Khloe, with a shudder. "Bites also seem to work."

"Anything that's infected gives off the slime. It can be pink, or purple. Pink for plants, and purple for animals. The explosions, though...I'd never heard of that until now. That's very disturbing."

"How did you escape your Bunker, then?" I asked.

"When the last helicopter took off, I wasn't even supposed to be on it. My father ran with me in his arms across the helipad with the monsters behind us. He threw me into the helicopter just as it was lifting up. Someone onboard grabbed me. I still remember my father's face as he fell away, as more of those things overwhelmed the tarmac. He was buried in a wave of them, his arms outstretched, screaming my name. I cried and cried, but we were already flying away.

"The journey to California was incredibly cold. We were supposed to join Bunker 114, but they didn't have room for us. So, we were to touch down in L.A.. The plan was for the Bunker survivors to find some uninhabited corner of the city and start new. But as we got closer, the helicopter blades just...slowed down. I don't know if we ran out of fuel or something else, but that next moment, we were spiraling toward the ground.

"We crashed. By some miracle, I survived. I was thrown out of the helicopter and landed in some grass nearby. I was knocked out, and woke the next day to find the helicopter turned on its side like some dead thing. Everyone else had died in the crash – all except me."

"Lucky."

"I know. My luck didn't end there, though. My older brother had escaped on an earlier helicopter that had flown to L.A. as well. I thought he had died."

"You're kidding."

"No. But it doesn't matter now, because he actually *is* dead now." She gave a long sigh. "That's another story."

"So, what happened after the crash?"

"I escaped, with nothing more than a broken collar bone and a few bruises. I ended up staying at the crash site for a day before heading into the ruins of the city. On my way there, a patrol found me, not from another Bunker like I thought. It was the Lost Angels."

"Lost Angels?"

"A gang. A man named Raine was their leader. He took me under his wing, and in time I forgot about my past. Soon, I was reunited with my brother, Samuel. He left the community the Bunker One survivors founded, and came to join us. A good thing he did, too. The Bunker survivors were taken and enslaved by the Black Reapers, another L.A. gang. They were our bitter rivals." Makara sighed. "That was twelve years ago. Another life."

"God...you must have been, what, seven or eight?"

"Seven. That's as much as I remember, anyway. I guess I was tough, even back then."

"Which makes you nineteen now?"

Makara nodded. "Nineteen. Nearly twenty. Point of the story is...yeah, you will cry sometimes. Life sucks, there's no way around that. But you never know when good might come. Maybe it won't, but you shouldn't count it out. And besides, that's what makes us human, right? Even if it seems impossible, even when there is no point; we fight to the death, with smiles on our faces."

I was quiet for a while. Hearing her story made me feel better, crazily enough – something I would have thought impossible just minutes ago.

"Thanks, Makara. Believe it or not, this actually helps."

"Get to bed, kid. Story time's over."

She lay down, and wrapped herself up. I heard her snores almost instantly.

I didn't know how she could fall asleep so fast. Despite my exhaustion, I lay there for a while, thinking. I thought about how narrowly I had escaped Bunker 108. I didn't know if I had it in me to survive another encounter with something infected with the xenovirus, human or not.

But at least I had Makara. Makara, who would teach me how to survive out here.

However, the more I saw of the Wasteland, the more I saw how the odds were stacked against me.

I just hoped I could find that fight within me.

Chapter 14

Makara and I woke with the sun. After eating, we set off. It was our goal to reach Oasis by nightfall.

Any tenderness Makara showed last night was completely gone. She did not smile, and her face assumed a hard, stony expression.

"This makes me nervous," Makara said.

"What?"

"It's so empty. No signs of human life."

"Isn't that normal?"

She shrugged. "I prefer to see my enemy."

"Do you think they're following us?"

"I *know* they're following us. Every batt we have is in that pack you're carrying right now. Brux is not going to let that go without a fight. Count on it."

I smiled. "I still can't get over the fact that you guys use batteries as money."

"They've been the currency of Raider Bluff for the last ten years. When you have a lot of goods going through a place, you need something to use as money, or things bog down."

"Raider Bluff?"

"It's the biggest city in the Mojave, on the Colorado River. Five thousand people, mostly slaves."

"Slaves?"

"It isn't pretty, but someone has to man the farms, or everyone starves."

"Still...who runs this place, anyway?"

"The Alpha. I haven't been to Bluff in a while, but last I went, the Alpha was a man named Char. I used to raid with him. He's a good man, for what good is worth around here."

"Why wouldn't he be Alpha anymore?"

"Because if you're Alpha for over a year, you're doing pretty damn well."

"Then why would anyone want to be Alpha?"

Makara shrugged. "Everyone thinks they're special, that they won't die from an assassination attempt."

It was hard to imagine how thousands of violent Wastelanders could cooperate long enough to build a city. But I guess even raiders needed a safe place to lay their heads for a while.

I guess there was a lot of things topside I'd have to get used to. Like, the fact raiders were tracking me because I was carrying a lot of batteries in my backpack. If only Makara knew how many rechargeable batteries there were in Bunker 108, she just might turn around and try to raid it.

"We better hurry, then," I said.

"We can only go as fast as our weakest link."

"What? Is this slow to you?"

"We should be running, given the circumstances."

"I can try harder, if that's what you..."

Makara held a hand up, and ducked. I fell to the ground with her.

"What is it?" I asked.

It was quiet for a moment. A gust of wind blew over the rocky ground.

"Nothing," Makara said. "Just a feeling."

"You fall to the ground because of a feeling?"

Makara stared pointedly at me. "You don't trust your gut out here, you're dead. It's a mistake most people only make once."

We waited a couple minutes. At least it was a chance to catch a breather.

I looked behind and saw nothing but the flat, red expanse we had already traversed. Some low hills rose on the southern horizon, along with several mesas against the backdrop of the sky, pink in the morning light.

It truly did seem like we were the only ones alive.

"We're not going to wait here all day, are we?" I asked.

Makara heaved an exasperated sigh. It looked like she wanted to hit me.

"Come on, brat."

We got up again, and headed in the direction we had been going.

"We have to be careful," Makara said. "There are only two of us, which makes us prime targets. Raiders go after the guaranteed kills. If I were raiding, my eyes would pop as soon as I saw us two walking across this plain."

We ascended a hill as we drew close to a narrowing in the valley, about a mile off. It was mid-morning. It seemed brighter than usual, for some reason. The weather had been more placid in the past couple days. Maybe the dying down of the wind affected how much dust stayed in the air.

Makara pointed ahead.

"See there, beyond that ridge of mountains?"

I could barely see them above the hills, but they were very tall.

"Yeah."

"Oasis is past them. It's just like it sounds. There's an oasis there, and a big town grew up around it."

As the morning went on, I thought of Makara, being a raider. I was traveling with a raider. Someone who had stolen. Someone who had killed.

Maybe someone who had murdered.

I didn't know why I was not afraid. I also didn't know why I was so quick to believe her story about Bunker One. Everything seemed to fit, I guess.

"So, why did you really decide to leave that group?" I asked. "It must've been pretty bad if you'd rather go with me."

"It was simple, really. Brux is a bad man, even for a raider. Most raiders kill because they must. Yes, raiding turns them bad. But Brux loves killing. He'll do it even when there's no reason to. Raiding is your only choice when you don't have a home. Most of these settlements won't take in outsiders. For good reason. Most outsiders are trouble. The settlements learned from their mistakes. Raiders will pretend to be nice, or hurt, or whatever, to get inside settlements and scout them. It takes an amazing feat to be accepted into a settlement these days. Either that, or plenty of batts. In a way, it just makes the problem worse. Good people who could contribute to settlements are turned away. They have to eat, too. So they become raiders."

"Is that what happened to you?"

Makara was quiet for a moment. "Sort of."

Suddenly, Makara stopped.

"What?" I asked.

She pushed hard down on my shoulder. Both of us fell to the ground and scurried behind a boulder. She held a finger to her mouth. She poked her head around, and quickly pulled it back. She rolled her eyes.

"I don't believe it..." she whispered.

"What?"

"Somehow, they got ahead of us."

Chapter 15

A gun went off, sending a spray of chipped rock at my face.

"I thought they were behind us!" I said.

"Same. They probably guessed where we were heading, and went to cut off the only way there."

"Where are they? I didn't see anything."

"There's an outcrop of rocks maybe a stone's throw away. I saw one of them behind one."

A few more bullets fired before a gruff male voice called them down.

It was dead quiet. Even the wind stopped. I could feel my heart beating madly in my chest.

Finally, the same gravelly, slimy voice who had called the shots off yelled out.

"Come out, Makara. We won't kill you. I promise. I just want the pack back. That's it."

Makara gave a savage laugh, loud enough for only me to hear. "Like we're going to fall for that."

"How the hell are we going to get out of this?" I asked.

She reached in her bag, and pulled out a canister with a lever.

"This should do the trick."

"What the..."

"Tear gas," she said. "I hope it's enough of a distraction."

"You *hope*?"

"If you got a better idea, I'd like to hear it. After a lob this, we'll take off for those hills to the east. On the other side, there's a trail that leads to Oasis."

I looked at the twisted hills uncertainly, not sure if there would be a way across. But what other choice did we have?

Makara pulled the plug on the tear gas canister, waited a couple seconds, and threw the damn thing over her shoulder. There were shouts of alarm, and then I heard a thud. Shortly after, the canister popped, and spewed gas into the air.

"Now," she said.

She sprinted from the shelter of the rock toward the hills. I took off after her.

I'd never run so fast in my life. I could hear the tear gas hissing behind us.

A few seconds later, the shots started.

I chanced a look back. There were five of them. Three of them, including Brux, were grabbing at their eyes, wailing in pain. The other two ran after us, rifles in hand.

"Run!" Makara yelled. "Don't look back!"

From time to time, a shot went off. A bullet whizzed past my ear. If I had been a few inches farther to the right, I would have been dead.

After a minute, we slowed from a sprint to a fast run. After a mile at this pace, I was ready to die. I was in decent enough shape...or at least, I thought I was. I was nothing compared to Makara. The only thing that kept me going was necessity.

Despite my lagging behind, we were gaining the lead. The backpack was heavy on me, and I felt it bobbing up and down on my shoulders. God, all this trouble for some batteries. I could hear them tinkle in time with my strides. It was like they were mocking me.

Makara had long slowed to a steady jog now, but I couldn't go on. I collapsed to the ground.

Makara stopped. "Sometimes, I forget you haven't walked more than a mile a day in your entire life, much less run one."

I was breathing too hard to protest. I felt like I was going to puke. Maybe I would have if there had actually been something in my stomach.

She took me by my sweaty palm.

"You need to get up," Makara said. She had already regained her breath.

I still lay on the ground, my pulse pounding in my brain. Finally, I let Makara pull me up. I walked beside her. She was still setting a fast pace, but I didn't complain.

We spent the rest of the morning climbing through the line of hills, trying to break out onto the other side. I looked back at the valley, but didn't see our pursuers.

"Are they going to follow us still?" I asked.

"Yes. If we can make Oasis, we should be safe."

"Great."

We found a pass, and worked our way through to the other side. When we made it, my breath caught in my throat. Before us, I could see a vast expanse of red going in all directions. In front of me, miles and miles out, was a sharp, jagged line of mountains. Their crowns were crested with snow. The entire flatland reflected a strange, golden glow.

A long, brown line snaked its way across the plain, close to the foothills. It took me a moment to realize it was the trail Makara spoke of. Along it I could see a long cloud of dust rising from the red earth.

"What is that?"

Makara squinted. "It's a caravan. Going to Oasis, from the looks of it."

"Maybe they can take us with them."

"Yes," Makara said. "Maybe they can. There is safety in numbers, after all."

Before I could say anything else, Makara was bounding down the hill. I hurried to catch up.

***

As we came closer to the dust cloud, I could see shapes moving within it. Then, I saw people, walking among animals laden with goods. The animals had long necks and long, brown hair. Each had a large hump on their backs.

"Are those...camels?"

Makara nodded. "Yeah."

"Camels...in California? Or was my Bunker actually built halfway across the world?"

"No. There were zoos before...you *do* know what those are, right?"

"I'm not an idiot."

Makara smirked, as if she might contend that. "There was a really big zoo in San Diego, which was not too far from here. Anyway, when Meteor crashed down, there was no one to take care of the animals. In the chaos, some escaped. Unlike most other animals, camels are built for harsh, dry environments. They would have thrived here even while everything else died off. I imagine the dry weather is their cup of tea." She shrugged. "That's my theory, anyway."

"Seems you have this well thought out."

Within a few minutes, we had caught up to the caravan. When we reached the road, several hundred feet behind the tail of the train, Makara raised her hands high.

"Do the same," she said. "They won't let us near till we check out."

"Check out?"

"We could be raiders to their eyes," she said. "Raiders attack caravans all the time, and sometimes use diversions. We could be a diversion, but we have to prove we're not raiders, or with raiders.

"Makara...are you going to get us killed?"

"No worries," Makara said. "I got this. They'll know I was with Raine when they see this..."

She lifted the left sleeve of her white tee, revealing a tattoo of a pair of angel's wings.

"Every Lost Angel has one, and they command respect, even out here in the Wastes."

Two men approached from the end of the train. They wore elegant, brown robes made from fine material. Each had a large hood drawn, masking their faces. Each had long, thick beards.

"Who are these guys?" I asked.

"That's a southern look," Makara said. "There's more cities in the south, and it's where most of the trade comes from."

"State your name and your business, travelers," one of them said.

"I'm Makara. This is Alex. We are traveling to Oasis, and wanted safe passage with your train."

"What business have you in Oasis, girl?"

"Raiders pursue us. We seek shelter with your caravan."

"Raiders? Are you with raiders?"

"No! I said they pursue us. If I were a raider, would I have this?"

Makara lifted her sleeve, revealing the Lost Angels' emblem.

The other man stepped forward, not seeming to care. "You invite danger to our trading party, and you wish to join us?"

"Look," Makara said. "They're in the area, and they will probably come after you, anyway. You might as well take us. We're both armed and good in a fight."

"How many are they?"

"Five. As of four hours ago, they were on the other side of those hills. Now, they could be anywhere."

I now noticed something among the pack animals that greatly disturbed me. The dust had settled a bit, revealing not only the animals and the robed and hooded figures leading them...but also humans, thin, stooping.

Chained.

"Makara..."

It appeared she noticed, too. Her face went white.

"These are slavers," she said.

Now, the hooded men seemed all the more sinister, and more filed our way. Some held rifles. I could count at least six of them.

"You travel to Oasis?" Makara asked. "Slavery is illegal there."

"Times are changing, girl. Raine is dead, and the L.A. gangs are always looking for fresh meat. Ohlan will let us stay there, with fair compensation, of course."

Both of the men stepped forward. Makara pulled out her handgun.

"Stop."

Instantly, four hooded men drew their own guns, pointing them at us.

"Put down your weapon, now," the man said. "This is our only offer."

"Let me make you an offer," Makara said. "You take one step closer and I'll blow your brains out. Now *back off*."

The man smirked, amused. His companion stood next to him, saying nothing. The other hooded men stood by, waiting for their master's order.

"It was nice knowing you, Makara," I said.

Then, the sound of a horn came from the caravan. The hooded men looked at each other.

Makara smiled. "Looks like you got some real raiders to deal with now."

Gunshots fired near the caravan. I could see men – the same men we had run from just hours before – running toward the goods-laden train.

"Defend the caravan!" the leader said.

It was amazing how quickly they turned from us. I guess, just this once, we were allowed to get lucky. Makara grabbed me by the arm.

"Now would be a good time to go," she said.

For what seemed the tenth time that day, we started running, away from the trail and into the desert to the east. After running about a mile, we slowed to a walk. We still heard the sounds of guns in the distance.

"No more running," I said.

"We need more distance," Makara said. "Brux might have seen us."

By now, the afternoon light was fading. When Makara saw me lagging behind, she knew she couldn't push me any farther. Off in the distance stood a little house. It looked so similar to the one we had stayed in the night before that at first I thought it was the same one. But, I knew it couldn't be because we were in a completely different area.

"Let's hope no one's home," Makara said. "I've never stayed out this far before. Hopefully, Brux and his gang don't know about this place."

When we arrived, the door was wide open. We went in, finding it empty and full of dust. Makara dropped her stuff on the floor, and I dropped mine nearby. I went back out on the porch, where two chairs were. I wrapped myself in my blanket, and sat.

"That doesn't look good," Makara said.

"What?"

She pointed toward the eastern horizon. I could see a wall of low mountains that seemed to be moving. Then, I realized they weren't mountains. They were clouds. Lightning flashed within them.

"Nasty one, from the looks of it," Makara said. "Better grab these chairs and step inside. It's going to be a long night."

"What is it?"

"A solid wall of dust and electricity. They'll kill you if you're caught in one. Lightning strikes, getting buried in sand, something heavy being thrown at you...they're called Devil's Walls for a reason."

"Will the house hold up?"

"Probably. It's seen hundreds of storms, I'll bet. But you never know."

"Comforting."

"Come on. Let's move."

The clouds were closer now. They moved incredibly fast. The last gleams of the fading sun cast pink, purple, and orange over it. The shifting of light and shadow, together with the lightning, gave it dangerous beauty.

Makara pulled me inside and shut the door tight.

Chapter 16

As soon as we were in, I collapsed on the floor.

"Hope the storm gets to Brux and the rest of them," Makara said. "That would make things a lot easier."

Makara and I sat in our chairs as the first wave of sand slammed against the house's eastern wall. From the groan of the wood, I thought it would cave in right there. But it held up, and only creaked.

From the windows, lightning flashed, so close I thought it would hit us. Living underground, I had never seen lightning. I didn't expect it to be so blinding and so...terrifying.

We ate a quick meal – the last of the rice bread, and some water, and went to sleep along the western wall.

Well, Makara went to sleep. It was much harder for me. The lightning and the storm were too much. The house was cold and pitch black, and I could only see when lightning flashed outside. I watched Makara's form, wondering how she could sleep through it.

Outside, the wind roared, and the temperature dropped until I could see my breath clouding the dry air. All I wanted was to be warm. The wind seeped through the cracks, and I could feel dust settling on my face, getting inside my mouth. My hands and feet were numb. Makara's breaths were still even with sleep.

"Makara?"

She didn't hear me. I got up, and began pacing the house. I was tired, sore, and cold – and, as always, hungry and thirsty. I wanted nothing more than to be back underground, where it was warm, where it was safe, and where there was always food. I would have killed for a hot shower.

I lay down again. If I had the guts, I would have woken Makara up and asked to share our blankets.

Finally, I was drifting off again. I was on the edge of dreams when a guttural scream shook entire frame of the house, jolting me awake.

Makara's eyes opened and she shot up from where she had been laying. She reached for her gun, and held it close. She looked at me and held a finger to her mouth.

"Don't move," she whispered.

I heard something, something *big*, scratching on the ground outside. It was barely discernible above the roar of the wind. I heard what I thought were heavy breaths. I hoped it was only the wind.

"It's one of them," she said.

"*Here?*"

We lay in the house, quiet. My heart was pounding. I hoped that if I breathed softly, if I didn't move, it would go away. The storm raged on outside. We waited for what seemed an hour.

We didn't hear the thing again.

"It is gone," Makara said.

"What could be that big?" I asked.

"I don't know," Makara said. "That virus can do weird things – make animals much bigger than they were meant to be. We must be near a Blight. Now, go to sleep."

I lay down, and closed my eyes. I didn't know how I *could* sleep with what she just told me. Yet, despite that scare, I found myself soon drifting off.

***

The next morning, we woke up late. The storm was over. Still, Makara told me to stay inside while she went to check things out.

A minute later, she came back in.

"There's nothing out there," she said. "We lost a lot of time yesterday, but we still might make Oasis by sundown if we hurry."

We left the house, and traveled all day without seeing another soul. It felt lonesome, out in the Wastes, but given what I'd seen of people out here, I guess that was a good thing.

We avoided the road and struck northeast, through the desert.

"Aren't there supposed to be cities around here?"

"Yeah, Oasis. Twenty miles."

"No. I mean, it's only been thirty years since Meteor, right? You'd think there'd be more buildings around."

"This area was pretty bare even before that."

"Still..."

"We're somewhere north of a city that was called Yucca. There are still signs of it, in some places. You can see buildings, half-buried in the dirt."

The day was warmer than yesterday, and the clouds were not as thick. They were still red – always red. And of course, there was not a trace of vegetation on the ground.

It seemed to be getting worse the farther we headed north. Smaller, then bigger, dunes rose from the earth. It was tough to climb them. Just seeing those dunes made me feel thirstier and more tired than I already was. We were rationing our water – there would be none until Oasis.

We never stopped, not even once as we plodded north. It no longer felt cold – in fact, I had broken into a light sweat. I was getting used to the work of walking, though there was a constant gnawing at my belly. The promise of a hot meal was all that kept me going.

We passed a few buildings on the way. We passed hills, rocky outcrops, but the day never brightened beyond noon. We were coming up a rise, when on the other side we came to a valley, covered with sand, surrounded in the distance by a ring of low, brown mountains. In the center of the valley I could see low wooden buildings crowded around a small lake. A circular, wooden wall surrounded the whole settlement.

We stopped, and I felt my heart swell with happiness.

"Oasis," Makara said. "It is good to see you."

It was thirty minutes before we were standing before the giant wooden gate. Two muscled guards sat in foldout chairs in the watchtower connected to it. Each had a rifle propped next to him. They scowled as we stopped before the entrance.

"Not looking good, Makara..."

"Quiet. You're making me nervous."

Neither of the guards said a word. One was tall and black, and chewed on a cigar, letting the ash fall to his feet. The other was tan with cropped, blonde hair. They stared down at Makara and me from their perch like vultures eyeing their next meal.

We stood there a while, Makara never breaking her gaze from the men after mine had long fallen to the sand.

Finally, the black guard spoke. "What do you want with us, raider? You know you and your ilk are unwelcome within these walls."

"I am not a raider," Makara said, her voice level. Her calm voice carried as well as a shout would. "Just a traveler, seeking a place to rest."

"Hmph." The guard smirked. "A likely story. Then the caravan leader, who now rests safely within our walls, must be lying. He saw you with the raiders yesterday. They made off with quite a bit of loot. I'm surprised your share wasn't great enough for you to come begging here."

"We oughta shoot you on sight," the blonde guard drawled.

The black guard smirked at that. I was ready to turn around. But Makara stood her ground.

"Let me speak to Elder Ohlan."

The black guard's eyes narrowed. "Elder Ohlan need not speak with scum such as you. I suggest you turn back. Now. Before I put a bullet in your chest."

"Ohlan knows me. And I knew Raine. I am Makara of the Lost Angels."

The guards exchanged curious looks. The blonde guard nodded, and the black guard turned to speak to Makara.

"Those are not light words you speak, Angel," the black guard said, adding a note of skepticism to that word. "Many would claim allegiance with the Angels. What proof do you have?"

"This," Makara said, lifting her sleeve.

The blonde guard fiddled with something behind him. A spotlight clicked on, sending a beam of bright light onto us. I held my hand to my eyes. Then, the light clicked off.

"Well enough, traveler," the black guard said. "If that work is false, then it is well done. I will tell Ohlan you are here. I will return when I have an answer."

The black guard left, while the other one stood watching, holding his gun and looking ready to use it.

"Don't say a word," Makara said softly. "With luck, Ohlan will remember me. The Lost Angels are still spoken highly of in the Wastes."

"Why are they so well-known?"

"Raine. He was not like the other gang lords. He was good. He helped people. He even helped build Oasis's walls. He's the reason the raiders don't own everything up to the border of L.A.."

We stood in front of the gate for a while. The blonde guard stood like a statue, paying no heed to our conversation.

"How do you know Ohlan, anyway?"

"I guess I forgot to tell you that part," Makara said. "Ohlan is Raine's brother."

Chapter 17

We waited a long time. With the night, came the chill, and it wasn't long before I was shivering. Makara gave a small hiss. I stopped.

Finally, the black guard came back

"You are to come in," he said. "Elder Ohlan wishes to speak with you."

The gate started to move. It creaked, rolling back inch by inch.

"First, you must surrender your weapons to me. They will be returned upon leaving."

Makara did so. I noticed, after giving up her first gun, she gave up another one from her pack.

"You have *two*? This whole time?"

She looked me up and down, and shrugged. "What of it?"

"I could use one, you know."

"Maybe in time," she said. "I'm surer about you, now."

I didn't understand why she kept it from me. Did she not trust me after all we'd been through?

The guard led us through Oasis's main drag. I'd never seen anything like it in my life. Buildings of sheet metal and wood, sometimes both, lined both sides of the street. From the sides people watched us, more people than I'd ever seen since leaving the underground. They were dressed in tattered, faded pants, colorless shirts, rarely of one piece, sewn together from a variety of different sources.

For the first time, I realized what a commodity clothes were, and how much I had taken them for granted living underground. All

Bunker residents had standard issue, wear resistant pants and shirts, along with camo and warm weather gear for recons. If anything needed to mended, there was the spare material to do so.

These people had no such luxury. They had whatever they found, or inherited it.

It wasn't just the clothes I noticed. The men had long, thick beards, and intense, dark eyes. The faces were gaunt and hardened, faces that were well beyond their years. There was little beauty left in the women, unless they were young. The harshness of life had taken it out early.

No one said a word to us. There was no greeting or welcome. There was just calculation in their eyes, wondering who we were, whether we were dangerous, whether we could be taken advantage of.

It was nothing like I had expected. These people were scraping to get by. I wondered if it was just the harsh environment and lack of resources, or the city's leadership. Either way, if this was the best a walled city had to offer, then maybe I didn't want it.

Then again, my hungry stomach disagreed.

"When can we eat?" I asked Makara.

"Just let me talk, and try not to get in the way."

We at last came to the oasis itself. There were palm trees around it, but they were shriveled and long dead. The whole thing was more like a pond than a lake. Buildings crowded around it, made from the same wood and sheet metal I had seen earlier.

All in all, the total population of the town might have been a thousand people.

One side of the oasis was completely bare. In the failing light it was hard to tell, but that might have been where the crops were.

A hooded figure stood, back to us, on the shore of the oasis. I knew this to be Ohlan, because two guards stood by him with rifles, facing toward us. He turned at our approach, lowering the hood. He, unlike the other people I had seen, was well-fed and his face clean-shaven. He was balding, with a ring of gray hair. He had a wrinkled face, in which was set a pair of sharp, blue eyes. There was toughness to him. Not the kind of toughness that comes from the hardships of life, but the kind of toughness that comes from inflicting hardships on others. I immediately did not like him.

"Elder," Makara said. "I thank you for this audience."

She knelt on one knee. I was shocked that Makara was kneeling to this guy who seemed to cover my soul in slime just by looking at him.

I felt I was expected to kneel, too. So I did. For Makara.

"No need for formalities," Ohlan said. His tone was cursory, and from it I deduced that there was, in fact, need for formalities. "Not between friends."

"Thank you, Elder," Makara said.

The guard who had escorted us stood by and watched like a hawk.

Now, Ohlan looked at me. I gazed for a moment into his cold, blue eyes before turning away as if burned. The eyes were shrewd, and seemed to catch everything I was in a moment. A contemptuous smirk played on his lips before he broke into a pleasant smile.

"Welcome, Makara of the Lost Angels." He looked toward me. "And who is this?"

"His name is Alex. He was alone, in the Wastes. He's with me now."

"Ah," Ohlan said. "The Wastes seem not to have yet chilled your heart, Makara. Perhaps there is a reason for this...adoption?"

"He was helpless. He is the only survivor of Bunker 108."

Ohlan flinched a bit. He quickly recovered, turning to me. "108? So Chan is dead?"

I stared at him, confused. What did he know of Chan? Of us? Apparently, Chan had more ties to the outside world than he had let on.

I swallowed my pride at having to answer this man. "I'm afraid so."

Ohlan's eyes narrowed. "An interesting development. How did it happen, if I may ask?"

I didn't want to tell him. But Makara and I needed him, as much as that hurt. He had control of this town and the food that would feed me tonight.

"A sickness," I said. "I barely escaped and would be dead if not for Makara."

"A sickness?" Ohlan considered. "Yes. There have been rumors of a new, wasting death. Agonizing. Bodies have been found over the last few weeks in the desert, bloated, ripped. The Blights ever spread."

Ohlan turned from me and back to Makara.

"Yes. I remember you. And I don't remember you. You are not the little girl who was Raine's own. You have changed. You were so happy and carefree, then."

"I had the luxury to be."

"Indeed. The City of Angels is no longer that. And the Angels are dead, and the cruel Wastes are now even crueler. You have hardened."

"I have become what I must."

"Indeed." Ohlan gave a coy smile. "Even so much as to take from others, I hope? You have not joined with the locusts of the east, have you?"

I had no idea what Ohlan was referring to, but then I realized he was talking about the raiders, and Raider Bluff.

"I became what I had to become, after Raine died," Makara said. "To survive."

"You should have come here first, Makara. You know I would have taken you in. But you didn't come. Are the walls of Oasis not sufficient for you? There was safety here, and family. But you chose another path. You became a raider."

Ohlan's eyes seemed to dance. Makara looked afraid. I felt protective of her. But what could I do? I was just a kid, and Ohlan was a powerful man.

"You said...family?" Makara asked.

"Oh yes. Did you not know?"

"Know? Know what?"

Ohlan smiled. "Your brother, Samuel. He was here."

Makara's eyes widened. "Samuel? Samuel, *my* Samuel, was here? When? Where is he now?"

Makara's hands shook from either nerves or excitement. I just hoped Ohlan wasn't lying. If he was, I was going to ring his neck, armed guards or not.

"He's gone, now," Ohlan said, turning around. "Samuel came here almost two years ago, thinking to find you here. But he did not find you here. He stayed on. About a year ago, he left to live at Bunker 114. Your brother has a brilliant mind, and Dr. Luken, the head of Bunker 114, wanted Samuel to help him with his research. Three weeks ago, Samuel returned from 114, intending to live here. He refused to say why, but apparently he had a falling out with Dr. Luken. It was only a few days later that we received a distress call from 114. Then, nothing. All of our transmissions have been met with silence. A few days later, Samuel led a patrol to 114 to find out what happened. He was supposed to have been back by now." Ohlan shook his head. "We have not heard from him since."

"Where is Bunker 114?" Makara asked. "We will leave immediately."

"114 is not far – it lies in the heart of Cold Mountain, about fifteen miles northwest."

"And he never returned?" Makara asked.

"No," Ohlan said. "After losing so many, I cannot risk more men and resources. In fact, I couldn't get anyone to go even if I wanted to. The widows still mourn the loss of their husbands. You can hear them weeping, in the night. And it's been such a cold, dry year. The crop is pitiful. Worse, those men had weapons and supplies with them, things that cannot be replaced." Ohlan sighed. "If only I could get them back."

"We will go," Makara said. "We will bring them back."

I looked at Makara, and looked at Ohlan. He gave a small, satisfied smile.

"Makara, I do not want to give you false hope. We have not heard from them since the day after they set out. Your brother..."

"...May still be alive. Even if he is dead, I need to know the truth. I couldn't live knowing he might be out there, still."

"Honorable. But what of your friend, here?"

"I will help her," I said. "These supplies must be very useful to you. Surely, you would like them back?"

Ohlan licked his lips. "Yes, of course I would."

"We will bring them back for you. In exchange, we would like to stay here, in safety."

Ohlan frowned. "Now, *that* is a lot to ask."

"What's the difference?" I asked. "You lost five, and you would gain two. Perhaps more, if there are any survivors. Furthermore, you would get the supplies."

Ohlan considered. I couldn't believe I was convincing him. Makara was quiet. Even she seemed impressed.

Ohlan nodded. "Very well. It is done. You can sleep here tonight. Ren will see to your meal, and give you enough for your journey there and back. You can start tomorrow morning."

"Thank you, Ohlan," Makara said. "We will not disappoint you."

Ohlan smirked. "Disappoint me? I have nothing to lose."

"We'll bring those supplies back. I'll make sure of it."

"And I hope you can find out what happened at 114," Ohlan said. "The supplies are most important, of course, but I would like to know what was strong enough to kill a patrol of my best men."

When Ohlan put it that way, going to Cold Mountain seemed like a bad idea. Yet, this was our only way into a safe home. And it was the only way Makara could find out about Samuel.

"Ren, show our guests to the common house."

Ren, the guard who had brought us here, saluted with his hand over his heart. "Yes, Elder." He turned to us. "Follow me."

We followed Ren down the road from which we came. The street was empty, though yellow lights illumined a building that seemed to be a saloon. Inside I could hear raucous laughter and booming, electronic music.

We walked until we stood in front of a sheet metal building along the wall.

"This is the common house," Ren said. "You will rest here tonight."

We went inside. The house was empty, and looked like it had not been used in a long time. Several rows of bunks lined one half of the room, containing dirty mattresses. Still, the prospect of sleeping on something other than rock or floor was good. The other half of the house contained a table. A large pot sat in one of the corners.

"What's that?" I asked.

Ren looked from me, to Makara, wondering if I was joking. "It's a piss pot."

Makara smiled at my embarrassment as Ren turned to leave.

"I'll be back with food," he said. "Ohlan wants you up and ready to go before dawn. You are not to leave this building until then."

"We don't plan to," Makara said.

When Ren walked out, we stashed our stuff by the bunks in the corner. Makara took my pack – the one with the batts in it, and hid it away under the corner bed where it would be out of sight.

We then went to the table, and sat.

"So, where did you get that extra gun?" I asked.

Makara turned back to me. She was tired, and did not look like she wanted to talk.

"It was for safekeeping," she said. "I did not know if I could trust you. I took it from Brux's pack after I knocked you out. I guess we'll be getting them back in the morning."

"Yeah. I guess."

"Look," Makara said. "I'm sorry. I see you're not going to try to shoot me with it, now. I'll give it to you tomorrow. Promise."

Makara seemed far away.

"How are you doing?" I asked.

"Just...shocked. Completely shocked. I thought he was dead these last two years. Now, he might be alive. Still, probably dead. But there is hope and I don't know what to do with it." She sighed. "I don't know if I can sleep tonight. My brother was all I had, Alex."

"He might still be alive," I said. "That would be something."

"I don't want to get my hopes up," Makara said. "I don't want this to be just another link on the chain of disappointments."

"Either way," I said. "At least we'll have somewhere to stay."

"Yes. But what's the point of being alive when you have nothing to be alive for?"

"Makara...wasn't it you who told me we go down fighting?"

She sighed. "Yes. But...I feel different now."

"That's all it is: a feeling. You never know what could be coming around."

"Sometimes, I feel like I'm just saying words. Words can't bring my brother back."

"Maybe we just have to believe. Even if it's in nothing."

"Believe in belief?"

"Maybe. Tomorrow, we will be closer to knowing the truth."

"That's what I'm most afraid of. I've lived my whole life the past two years on the assumption that he's dead. What will he think of me and what I've done to survive? I did all those things because I didn't care. But now, maybe I do."

"There is a time for that," I said. "But it is not now. Now, we have a chance to rest. So let's do that."

We sat there for a few minutes. Makara calmed down. Somehow, my words had done the trick.

Weird thing is, I wasn't sure how much even I believed in them.

I thought about Ohlan. Living here under the dominion of that man seemed an evil fate in and of itself.

"Was Ohlan always like this?"

"Yes. He is a smart man, but he is also cruel. But it is his cruel and calculating ways that helped him to build Oasis. People follow him without question. If they didn't, they would be ostracized, which is as good as death."

"I almost don't want to stay here," I said. "But it's hard to argue with a full stomach. It doesn't have to be forever, I guess."

We still had the batts. Surely, that had to be worth something somewhere. We could always find another town.

At that moment, the door opened. Ren walked in, carrying two steaming trays of food. My mouth watered, and my stomach growled.

He set the trays on the table.

"There is a well behind the house, near the wall," he said.

Ren left without another word.

"Charming," I said.

"This place does not like strangers, that is for sure." Makara stood. "I'll go fill our canteens. You can start eating without me."

"No. I'll wait."

It was a minute before she returned. Sitting there with that steaming tray of potatoes, beans, and corn was torture.

As soon as she got back, I dug in.

When you go for a while without eating much, you get full fast. I had to force myself to finish, and I felt like my stomach was going to explode. Makara was right; hunger is the best seasoning. I couldn't remember a better meal in my life.

After gulping down my water, Makara and I sat for a moment. We were both tired, not saying anything. She wanted to be alone with her thoughts. So I went to my bunk in the corner, got out my blanket, and hunkered down for the night.

The mattress might have smelled funny, but it was soft and comfortable. I closed my eyes, and dreamed of a future that did not involve getting shot at, living on the run, with a full meal every night and at least some semblance of routine.

Only thing was, I was probably going to die before any of that happened.

Chapter 18

After getting the guns back, we left Oasis at dawn by the north gate past all the fields. On our way, we passed wheat and corn stalks, half withered by the harsh, dry environment. It was a wonder that anything at all could grow out here.

Then, we were out in the Waste again, heading northeast to Cold Mountain, a shadowy mass in the distance. It was surrounded by smaller mountains. I wondered how we'd find Bunker 114 in that entire thing.

It was still dark, and we saw no hint of the sun until a golden glow shone above the eastern mountains. The desert floor was bathed in a vibrant, orange hue.

On the way, Makara handed me my gun. My gun. It felt good to even think those words.

We stopped for a short break so I could get to know it better. It was a Beretta handgun. It looked at least fifty years old, but it had a lot of character. It had many scratches and scuffs from the years, and the design was sleek and round.

Makara took a moment to show me how to use it. She took out the magazine. Fully loaded, it contained seventeen rounds. Makara showed me two boxes of 9mm rounds in the pack. The two boxes each contained a hundred rounds. I had plenty of ammo as long as I didn't get too trigger happy.

When I latched the holster onto my belt, words cannot describe how much more secure I felt.

We walked on.

"How far do you think it is?" I asked.

"Ten miles or so," Makara said. "It's still morning, so we're making good progress."

As the sun rose higher in the sky, the mountain appeared to get a little closer. It wouldn't be long, now.

We walked on at a fast pace the rest of the day. By late afternoon, we had entered the foothills of Cold Mountain. It rose up in front of us like a giant tooth, wicked looking. It had a long, pointed top, like a spire. It was hard to see the top, as it was mostly lost in reddish haze.

I noticed something else, too, as we drew close. The sides of the mountain were purple, pink, and burnt orange.

"What is that?" I asked.

We both stopped to look at it. It was clear that the color was unnatural. Multicolored layers of something toppled down the mountain in frozen waves. It looked alive.

"A Blight," Makara said. "No wonder that patrol did not come back."

"Are they always dangerous?"

"I've never seen one this big," she said. "It's taking up the whole mountain. You never know what kind of things you can run into in a Blight."

"Monsters?"

"Just be ready. Shoot anything that moves."

***

We were almost to the northern face of Cold Mountain. Nothing had jumped out at us, yet, but being in my first Blight was a nerve-wrecking experience. The entire ground was coated in a thick, sticky purple and pink substance. This, I knew, was xenofungus. I had only seen samples in my father's lab. To see miles upon miles of it was surreal and frightening. It squished as we walked on it.

Pillars, maybe ten to twenty feet tall, rose from the purple stuff in organic towers. They appeared to be spawned by the stuff on the ground, and had massive, bell shaped openings that dripped pink slime. The slime flowed downhill, pushed along by the fungus. It collected toward the end of the Blight. It might have been the way the fungus spread ever outward.

We worked our way through the towers and spongy ground. It was late afternoon by now. We had found no Bunker entrance, so far. But I knew we would have to find it quick. Getting caught out here at night was a terrifying thought.

We turned the corner of the mountain to find ourselves on its northern face. The entire side was covered with purple and pink grime. It glowed from the hazy, setting sun, and clouds of insects swarmed near the towers. Right in the middle of it all was a gaping maw, black, lost in shadow.

"That looks promising," Makara said.

"Like the mouth of a beast."

"If there's any entrance, that will be it. Come on. It's not far."

As we crossed the purple field, I couldn't shake the feeling that we were being watched. I looked around, but saw nothing.

"I have a feeling something is watching us..." I said.

Makara stopped. "I don't feel anything..."

I turned around. I could see nothing but multicolored miles of Blight, spreading in all directions.

When I turned around again, they were right in front of us.

Two dog-like creatures, completely hairless, were kneeling in front of Makara. In tandem they pounced on her, and she fell backward. She screamed, dropping her gun. Their jaws snapped, closer to her neck. She elbowed one in the head.

I ran forward, pulling out my Beretta. I fired at the one about to finish Makara. Two bullets plowed into the head. The thing yelped and went slack, purple goo oozing from the wounds.

The other monster snarled as it turned to face me. I fired several times, the bullets tearing into its chest and front legs. I couldn't get a steady shot.

It gave a shrill shriek as it lunged for me. It had me on the ground against the slimy fungus. Its completely white eyes bored into mine. I could feel drool dripping on my neck, stinging on contact.

Another gunshot. I felt the creature's weight collapse onto me. I pushed it off in a panic, and reached for my neck, wiping the drool off with my hands.

"Wash it off," Makara said, handing me her water bottle.

"Thanks."

Makara was still recovering her breath. "Thanks, yourself. That was some shot. I would have been dead."

"Same for you."

I poured the water on my neck, wiping it dry with my shirt.

Makara looked at it closely. "The skin's a bit red. But there's no open wound. You'll be fine."

"Are we good to go, then?" I asked.

"Yes. We should have seen those coming. Unfortunately, they blend right in."

We walked the rest of the way to the cave. We now stood in front of it. The air smelled cool and damp, and carried the faint smell of rot. It was hard not to feel like we were walking into some horrible creature's mouth as we walked down the slope, into it.

When we were a good ways in, Makara retrieved a flashlight, and clicked it on.

In front of us were the dead bodies of the lost patrol.

"Oh no..." Makara said, rushing forward.

They were utterly mutilated. From head to toe, something really big had treated these people like rag dolls. A bloody head lay in a corner, surrounded by a ring of pink fungus that seemed to be feeding off it. The rest of the body parts had been gathered in a twisted, gory corpse pile.

Makara went toward it. I grabbed her by the hand.

"Are you crazy? Don't go near that."

Makara stopped. "You're right. But he might be..."

Might? He probably was. But I wasn't going to say that to Makara. The bodies were not just ripped up. They were rotting. They had suffered through at least a week of decomposition, and the way the fungus fed off them just made recognition all the more difficult.

"If there are any survivors, they either escaped or ran deeper into the cave," I said.

We spent the next few minutes gathering supplies of the lost patrol. Guns, ammunition, medicine, food...it was a treasure trove. I could see why Ohlan wanted this stuff back. I tried my best to ignore the dead bodies.

Makara was barely holding it together. There would be time for grieving, later.

"Look, Makara...we have maybe an hour of sunlight left. We need to hurry."

She nodded. "I know. I'm trying. Just...let me work, okay?"

After five minutes, we had gathered all we could into two large backpacks we had found nearby. It was almost all the stuff, including the guns and ammunition.

"Alright," I said. "Let's go."

Suddenly, the cave darkened. At first, I thought Makara had turned off her flashlight. But she reached for her gun, and that's when I heard a bullet.

I turned to the mouth of the cave, and saw five figures blocking the entrance.

"Hey, Makara," came that nasty, gravelly voice. "You miss me?"

It was Brux.

***

"Run!" Makara yelled.

We didn't turn to look back as they fired at us. Bullets whizzed by. Makara turned off her flashlight, and the darkness swallowed us.

"I'll find you, Makara!" Brux yelled. "I'll track you down if it's the last thing I do!"

His voice was lost as we ran on. After running and tripping for a minute, Makara turned the light back on – it was just too dangerous not to see where we were going, especially when something much worse than raiders lived here.

We rounded corners, sloping ever downward. A thin trickle of a stream collected at our feet, and we splashed our way through the darkness.

The light revealed scenery more and more alien to the eye. Pink and purple fungus hung in stalactites. There was a curious, deadening of all sound from the purple stuff covering the walls. A pungent, sickly sweet smell burned my lungs.

Soon, it was hard to breathe.

"Makara," I said, stopping.

She looked back. "We can't stop now."

My head swam. It was hard to focus.

I felt a hand slap my cheek.

"Wake up, damn it!" Makara yelled. "Do you want to die here?"

I pushed forward one step. I heard voices behind us in the distance, from a different world.

I fell to my knees.

"Go on, Makara..."

She didn't go on, either. Her eyes grew hazy, and she fell to the ground.

"What...is this...?"

My only desire was to lie on the bed of fungus we were now on. It was so soft. I nestled in it. It was warm, and damp, like a living thing. I felt like I would soon become a part of it. I wanted nothing more than that.

I felt it itching on my face. But I didn't care.

Makara and I were soon fast asleep.

Chapter 19

I swam through dreams – peaceful dreams, the kind you never want to wake from. I saw my father, Khloe, and even my mother. It had been so long since I'd seen her. She had brown hair, and soft, kind eyes. How this was her, I didn't know – it had been so long since she had died.

After what seemed days in this state, even the dreams began to fade.

I opened my eyes and found myself in a dark room, alone. I was on a small bed, and I made out the faint outlines of a desk in the corner.

I thought I had died.

I tried to move my legs, but they didn't obey my commands.

"Makara..."

My voice was soft and raspy. Nothing answered it.

Then, the door opened, letting in a flood of white light. I saw a shadowy shape enter. I shielded my eyes.

"You are up, finally," came a deep, male voice.

"Who are you?"

I did my best to sit up, and leaned my back against the headboard of the bed. I was terribly thirsty.

"Water."

The man handed me a leather canteen. I drank the warm water greedily.

"I found you and Makara while collecting samples," he said. "Foolish thing – to run into a xenofungal field without the proper breathing equipment. If I hadn't come along, you would have been dead. Or worse."

My eyes were starting to focus. I could now see that the man tall, all angles and hard muscle. He had broad shoulders, tanned skin, and a shaved head. His eyes, while I could not determine their color, were focused and serious. He looked to be in his early to mid-twenties.

"How long have I been here?" I asked.

"I found you on September 30. It is now October 2. Some never wake from the coma caused by xenofungal sleeping spores. You were lucky. I came along just in time. Some luck that was."

"Where is Makara?"

"She awoke earlier in the day, but I couldn't get two words out of her. She is asleep again. She will be fine."

He walked to the door, flipping on the light. Suddenly, everything was illuminated, and my eyes burned.

The man looked very familiar. At first, I thought I might have known him from Bunker 108. He would have been a security officer, given his stature. But I knew for a fact he wasn't from 108. I would have remembered him.

Then, I realized he looked like Makara.

"Samuel?"

"Yes. You must be Alex."

"How do you know that?"

"It's the only name Makara keeps saying in her sleep. That, and mine."

"We thought you were dead. You were the whole reason for our coming here."

He gave a small smile. "Was I now?"

"Makara will go crazy. Are there other survivors?"

"No. Just me."

"We were chased by raiders into the cave. We thought you were dead when we saw the corpse pile."

Samuel nodded. "They ran you right into the Bunker, then. You are lucky you survived."

"How did you escape? What happened to you guys?"

"We will speak of that later. Let us go check on my sister."

"Is she awake?"

Just then, she screamed from the room next to us. Samuel and I got up and ran out of the room, pistols in hand. I ran after him.

We went into the hall, and burst into Makara's room. Makara was sitting up in bed, eyes wide.

"Makara, what's wrong?" Samuel asked.

Makara's eyes looked at Samuel as if he were a ghost. She didn't say a word.

Samuel went to her, grabbed both her hands, and helped her out of bed. All the time, Makara never looked away, not believing.

There was still no discernible reaction in Makara's face. Then, slowly, her eyes filled with tears, and her shoulders shook.

Samuel embraced her. Makara let out a suppressed sob.

"I can't believe this," she said. "It is too good to be true."

"It is true," Samuel said. "I am here. Believe it."

They parted.

"First," Makara said. "What about those raiders? Did they follow us in?"

Samuel shook his head. "I saw no raiders. I guess they did not follow you in. Though I would not have been surprised if they had, given the contents of Alex's pack."

"They might still be out there," I said.

"Maybe," Samuel said. "But it's been two days now. Unless there was another reason, they would have long given up the chase by now."

"They probably took all the supplies we left at the front of the cave," Makara said.

She looked at Samuel as if she still could not believe her eyes.

"And in either case," Samuel said, "there is another way out. It is harder, and it comes out near the top of Cold Mountain. There is an elevator shaft, but to get there we would have to go through the thickest part of the Bunker. The part that is not secure."

"Can't we just go out the way we came in?" I asked. "You have breathing masks, don't you?"

"Just the one," Samuel said. "I have turned this section of the Bunker up and down looking for more since you've been sleeping, but have found nothing. We'd have to search the main part of the Bunker – at which point we might as well just leave through the elevator shaft. We haven't the time or the resources to secure the whole thing."

"Are we leaving now?" I asked.

"No," Samuel said. "You and Makara need rest. We can catch up in the meantime."

"Not before we have something to eat, Sam," Makara said.

"Yes," Samuel said. "I'd forgotten that. The kitchen is just across the hall. There is still plenty of frozen food. The microwave still works."

We went there, and had a meal of chicken, vegetables, and bread, which had all been frozen in the deep freeze. I hadn't had meat since Bunker 108, and it tasted amazing. By the time we finished, I was ready to sleep again. But Samuel instead led us down the hall, and into a small break room with some sofas, a television, and a pool table.

"We can speak here. First things first - what happened to you after Los Angeles, Makara?"

Up to this point, I had not heard the full story. I was listening almost as eagerly as Samuel.

She began.

***

"It was two years ago." Makara smiled grimly. "The day Raine was assassinated. It was my last hour in Los Angeles. It was a warm day. You might remember that, Samuel. I was on the roof of the Lost Angels Headquarters, the main base of operations for the gang. It used to be a thirteen story bank just west of downtown. Now, I suppose it is still only rubble.

"I was watching the sunset from the rooftop when the streets came alive. Hundreds of Black Reapers surrounded the tower. You ran to the roof, screaming for me. You told me Raine was dead, and that we had to leave. You ended up staying, however." She sighed. "I still haven't forgiven you for that.

"You pushed me out the back door, with a pack and a gun. Then, a few mortars flew through the air, whistling as they passed. The explosions rocked everything, and all I saw was darkness and fire. Acrid smoke filled my lungs, stung my eyes, choked my breath. My hearing faded, and then there was nothing – I felt nothing, saw nothing, knew nothing as the rubble crashed down."

She said nothing for a while. Samuel and I waited for her to go on.

"The entire building was a ruin behind me. It was only as the gunshots faded, as the Reapers' bikes tore through the streets and surrounded the building, that I ran. I ran as far as I could, though I had nowhere to run to. I ran east through the streets, through decaying buildings, through toppled fences and broken walls. I looked back, and the tower was gone in a smoking ruin, along with my entire life. I thought you had died.

"I wandered for weeks. Some nights I found food. Some nights I didn't. Winter was coming.

"It was the next day when I fell in with a group of raiders. At first, one of the men wanted to use me and keep me as his. But I shot him. I didn't care what they did to me. The leader – a man named Char – smiled. He fed me, and put clothes on my back.

"I was in.

"We raided all through autumn. We killed, we stole, and the men did worse. But never once would they touch me. I was one of them.

"I was aware that I was becoming less and less of a person. But I felt less than nothing. By October, we headed west out of the valley along I-10, into the Mojave. We traveled for weeks, until we reached Raider Bluff. I had never seen anything like it. The city is huge, built on a giant, three-tiered mesa. The city has three levels, including the fortified Alpha's Compound at the top. We came, laden with camels of goods. We were treated like kings. I allowed myself a smile, then. With my share of the loot, I was able to trade for guns, for food, for clothes, and batts. It was all mine.

"Everyone in town wanted to know who I was – the woman raider. The women in Raider Bluff are little more than slaves for the men. There are exceptions – like my friend Lisa, who runs a bar called the Bounty, who I became friends with. When winter came on, I hardly stepped outside from that place. It was cold, but I stayed in there, where I rented a room. I drank much. I hardly remember the winter of 2058.

"When the storms ended, raid leaders searched for new recruits. Dozens approached me, but I turned them all down. I intended to stay there and drink myself to death.

"And then, I realized my batts were running thin. Without the batts, I could not eat, and more importantly, I could not drink. I decided to continue living. I don't know why. I didn't have anyone. Everyone in my family was dead. I knew nothing of friendship.

"I entered onto a raid with the next leader who approached me. His name was Brux."

Makara paused to drink from a glass of water. She looked at me, and gave a tired smile.

"Brux was especially cruel, even for a raider. His specialty was slaves. Women, mostly. I did not know this at the time. Lisa warned me against him, but I did not care. I knew he brought back the loot, and I wanted that.

"That year, I saw the most terrible things. I will not repeat them here. I felt myself die more and more each passing day. I was afforded no respect among the raid group, and the only way I could get it was by killing one of them who tried to rape me. Finally, they learned, and kept away from me. Many times, I flew into rages and threatened to take my share back to Bluff. Brux would not hear of it.

"I became aware of it, slowly. Brux would watch me on those cold nights, when he thought I was sleeping. Countless times he tried to have his way with me. I learned to both sleep and be aware of the danger. But he never let me be, no matter what I tried. I could not kill him – that would be mutiny, a crime punishable by crucifixion. I had seen a death like that, in the winter. The crows had feasted well all the next day.

"I thought the year would never end. It was a good year, though, if good could be used as a word. Twenty slaves, one hundred camels, and plenty of loot. I collected four times the batts with Brux than I did under Char.

"How could I do this, you ask? I don't know. I had no conscience, then. I didn't care about anything."

Makara had stopped talking. Samuel had become distant – grieved, in a way. I felt like I had to say something, to make her go on.

"What caused you to care?" I asked.

"That did not happen until the next season. There are two seasons in Raider Bluff – winter, and summer. In the summer, you raid. In the winter, you hide inside and try not to freeze to death. That winter, the end of 2059, I told Lisa I was done. But I could not be done. We both knew this. Raiding, once chosen, could never be abandoned. One, because no settlement will take you. And two, once abandoned, even raiders won't have you. You either raided, or you starved. It was that simple.

"And there was something else I did not know. Brux had marked me. It was believed, however falsely, that I was his woman. The other raid leaders were afraid of him, so they did not ask me to raid with them next season. There was nothing but to go with Brux again that summer.

"When we left Bluff, things went well at first. And then – misfortune upon misfortune. A sandstorm killed two men and buried the first two months of loot. We spent days trying to dig it up, but we had lost it. After that, everything was lean."

"Lean?" I asked.

"Had been picked over already. No loot." She sighed. "We trekked north, far from normal raiding territory. For miles and miles we walked, until we reached the Ice Lands. Though it was summer, the nights were deathly cold. But Brux was a risk-taker – he thought there would be people here, or at the least, cities that had not yet been looted. We were trying to find one – called Portland, but we became lost in a Blight.

"This was my first Blight to see on the West Coast. The trees were twisted and turned. I had seen nothing like it since my original home – Bunker One. One night, we were attacked by a pack of monsters. We killed them, but at great cost. What men did not die in the attack froze or starved on our journey back to southern lands. Somehow, we found our way back – just six of us, out of an original twelve.

"In southern lands again, we found food, but little else. Whatever we raided became lost, or went straight to Brux.

"We were on I-10, along the caravan routes, hoping for a lucky train that another raid hadn't yet gotten. But instead, we came upon a sick man – a government man, because he wore a Bunker 114 uniform.

"Brux stabbed him, and we dragged him off the road and left him for dead. Little did we know that we were so close to Bunker 108. That Bunker ended up taking him in, and that man spread the

Blight sickness to everyone there."

"Wait," Samuel said. "Bunker 108 is gone, too?"

I nodded. "It is. I am the only survivor."

Samuel looked at me with pity. I tried to ignore that.

"So, going there is no longer an option," Samuel said. "I had hoped to learn more from a certain Dr. Keener. Did you know him?"

A flood of emotion overwhelmed me when I heard that name. "He was my dad," I said.

Samuel's eyes widened. "Really? I am deeply sorry. He was a scientist, wasn't he? He studied the xenovirus."

I nodded. "He did. He knew a lot, but I don't know as much about it. How do you know about him?"

"Everyone who has spent any amount of time in Bunker 114 is aware of Dr. Keener's research. From time to time, notes would be sent back and forth between us."

"Why were you hoping to speak with him?" I asked.

"To learn more about this xenovirus...I had hoped..." Samuel shook his head. "I'm sorry, Alex. I will not speak of it anymore."

"It's fine," I said.

Makara waited a moment, before picking up where she had left off.

"After the incident with the sick man, we headed toward Raider Bluff. We camped on some hills, and waited by the Twin Routes, as we had in the old days. We might yet come back to trade for enough batts to last the winter.

"But that night was unusual, because Brux slept deeply. It was even more unusual when I saw a boy crawling into our camp. You can imagine my surprise. My eyes half-opened, I watched as he crept up to Brux's backpack, picked it up, and simply walked off with it. The backpack with all the batts and Brux's reserve weapon. Instead of stopping him, I let him go. He disappeared into the darkness. I waited. Then, I saw my chance to get out of there. If the boy could share the batts with me, then I could buy my way into one of the towns and never have to raid again. It was a gamble, but my life was not getting any better.

"I left the fire, and the raiding life forever. And here I am now, speaking to my brother."

Makara then went on to explain everything we had gone through...how Brux had attacked us again, the attack on the caravan, the sandstorm and the monster that had been outside, the meeting with Ohlan, and our agreement to find the lost patrol and recover its supplies in exchange for citizenship in Oasis – all up to meeting Samuel.

Next, I told my story – a little of my life in the Bunker, and what had happened with the infection. I kept it brief. Though it was hard, I talked about losing both my father and Khloe. Samuel seemed especially interested when I talked of my father's research into the xenovirus. I told him what I knew, however little it was. Samuel nodded, as if he had heard most of it already.

"I have read all of your father's research," he said. "He makes some interesting observations on the evolution of the xenovirus. Tell me, did he..."

"You've made him talk enough, Samuel," Makara said. "He needs to recover from the week he's had."

I couldn't argue with that. It was all I could do not to fall asleep on the couch.

"Alright, then" Samuel said. "We'll sleep. In the morning, I can tell you about what I've found out since being here."

We each went to our rooms, and to our beds. I was asleep as soon as my head hit the pillow.

Chapter 20

I slept fully and deeply. When I awoke, I was sore all over – especially my legs, which felt like jelly. I stretched them out, and headed to the kitchen to find some breakfast.

As I was warming up a ration in the microwave, I frowned. A trail of water led from the hallway into a room on the other side of the kitchen. It definitely wasn't there yesterday.

I left the hum of the microwave behind, and went toward the door. It was open a crack, and dark inside. I paused a moment before tapping it open.

The door opened slightly. Inside, I could see a form.

It was Makara, toweling herself off after clearly taking a shower. She was facing away from me, and was naked and dripping wet. I panicked and backed out just as she started to turn.

I didn't think she saw, but I felt horribly awkward. I hadn't realized that was where she was staying. She had been in a different room yesterday.

I went back to the kitchen, embarrassed, where the microwave was now beeping. I took out my food. I looked back at the door. Makara was still in there.

She emerged, wearing new clothes – camo pants and a black tank top. Her hair was still wet. She wore a knowing smirk.

"Showers are down the hall," she said.

I fumbled my tray, nearly spilling my food on the floor. "Yeah. Okay."

She looked at me, shaking her head. "You're so cute when you're embarrassed."

"I...I didn't know you were in there. I'm sorry. I just saw the water..."

She rolled her eyes. "Shower up. Samuel's already in the break room. I think he wants to get started."

"Am I the last one up?"

"Yes. We don't have a lot of time, so try to hurry."

"You guys could have woken me up."

"We tried. Twice. Like talking to a rock."

I felt myself go red. "Fine. Just..."

She raised an eyebrow.

"I'll meet you there, then," I said.

I practically swallowed my food and headed for the showers. I let the cold water run over me for about two minutes before the shock of it made me step out. I couldn't even get suds. Still, it was better than nothing.

While showering, I realized I'd forgotten to find some new clothes. However, after getting out, I found a clean set waiting for me on the bench. Makara had snuck in without me realizing it.

I put on the clothes. They fit remarkably well. I guess she had checked me out, at least a little bit, to know what would fit me.

I went into the break room, where Makara and Samuel were already waiting. As soon as I sat, Samuel began his story.

"I escaped Lost Angel Headquarters using an underground tunnel. It was hard to pull myself from the rubble, but I managed it. Raine was dead, and you were gone, so I had nothing there.

"I tried to find you, Makara. I went to every settlement in southern California, but none of them had seen you. After a year I had to face the truth...you were gone.

"Finally, I settled in Oasis. Ohlan was Raine's brother, so I thought it might go well for me there. This was far from the case. I was unhappy. Ohlan runs it like a cult. There have been...killings. I felt I could not escape. At least, not until I was presented with the opportunity.

"One day, a patrol from Bunker 114 came by, led by a man named Dr. Luken. A few times a year, Bunker 114 would make contact in order to trade supplies. Ohlan had me stay with him as he brokered a deal between Oasis and 114.

"After the meeting, I introduced myself to Luken, telling him about my escape from Bunker One. When he heard of my firsthand experience with the xenovirus, he told me of Bunker 114's research into it. I expressed interest in helping with their efforts. Luken offered me a position, and I accepted.

"Ohlan was not happy to see me go, but it was exactly what I needed.

"Over the next year, I learned much about the xenovirus. While the basic structure of it is the same, there are various strains – each strain affecting a different species, from microbes to, now, human beings. New strains were always being discovered in the wild. I would often go out to collect samples – there was a Blight about ten miles north of us.

"I've noticed a pattern over the past year, however: the xenovirus was increasingly affecting more complex organisms. I knew from my experience at Bunker One that the xenovirus affected animals. However, I had never seen it here, in California.

"There were several connections we made – the bigger the Blight, the more complex its ecosystem. Bigger Blights are older, meaning the xenovirus has had more time to evolve and affect greater amounts of life forms. The infestation to the north was growing ever larger, until even the animals were becoming infected.

"We saw great threat in this. Bunker 114, and even Oasis, would be in grave danger at current Blight expansion rates. Our research then switched focus from trying to understand the virus to trying to eradicate, or at least reverse it.

"As part of our research, we brought back a live rat specimen that was infected with the disease. Collecting one was difficult and dangerous, but ultimately successful. It was a nasty creature: hairless, pink, sticky skin, and totally white eyes. The turned rat was brought back to 114 and given into the care of a woman named Kari Wilson."

Here Samuel paused, and gave a long sigh, as if dreading the part that came next.

"Dr. Wilson was a brilliant scientist, and my friend. One day, while transferring the rat to another cage, it escaped and bit her. We thought it was nothing at first. But then she became sick within hours. Apparently, whatever strain of the xenovirus that affected that rat could also affect humans. She left early that night to go to bed.

"That morning, she did not join us at breakfast. Me and someone else went to check on her in her room." Samuel hesitated a moment before going on. "We knocked, but there was no answer. Finally, we opened the door. Kari was laying still, her face completely pale, her eyes open. I knew, without even feeling her pulse, that she was dead.

"We immediately quarantined her. We thought long on where to put her, but we eventually decided to cordon off an area in the labs that was not used often.

"Dr. Luken wanted to do an autopsy. I protested, but most of the other scientists wanted to know what happened.

"So she was there, in the operating room. I could tell she had visibly changed, even from that morning. All her hair had fallen out, and her face became deathly pale, revealing black veins beneath cadaverous skin.

"It became clear that she was not truly dead – her arms and legs began to twitch. There was hope that she might be saved." He sighed. "Obviously, we were wrong."

Samuel stopped talking. I thought he might go on, but what he had said so far had emotionally drained him. I wouldn't be the one to push him on under those conditions.

Just when I thought he wouldn't speak again, he willed himself to continue.

"What resulted was madness," Samuel said. "They were able to restrain her, but she had fallen under the full influence of the virus. She was put in the holding cell, originally designed for prisoners. Dr. Luken told us that we were going to study the effects of the xenovirus on Dr. Wilson."

Samuel shook his head. "Most agreed with him. I, and a few others, did not. I was the only one to leave. That is why I am the only one alive today. I went to Oasis, but kept everything to myself.

"Days later, Oasis received a distress call from 114. There were sounds of struggle, and then silence.

"I knew what had happened, but Ohlan insisted on sending a team to investigate. Five other men and I were selected for the task.

"Even in the few days I had been away, the infestation had grown exponentially. Xenofungus covered the entire north face of Cold Mountain.

"The mission was a disaster. Kari ambushed us at the entrance of the cave. There, I got my first look at her. She had grown to twice her size, probably from having fed on the scientists who lived in 114. Whoever she had been was gone, now. Her face was twisted, grotesque, and she stank of death. Blood and flesh stained her mouth, where long, sharp teeth protruded. She had long claws, extending from elongated fingers. And those eyes – I will never forget those completely white eyes staring into me.

"I was only able to escape by running into the cave, toward the Bunker. There was another with me...but he did not get his mask on in time when we reached the area with the fungal spores. He was knocked out, and Kari dragged him away.

"I ran into the Bunker, right to the dorms. There was only one entrance and exit, so I sealed the door, and locked it tight.

"That was two weeks ago. I've been here ever since. The power still works, and there is enough food to last me months. I thought of leaving earlier, but I wanted to take the opportunity while I was here to learn more about what happened after I left.

"In the research database, I found Doctor Luken's research notes – the first description, however brief, of the human xenovirus.

"The notes detailed Kari's transformation from human to...something else. Infection, sickness, followed by a comatose state, then a reawakening brought about by a physical stimulus. It was noted, even after the transformation, that Kari would not move unless she there was something alive in the vicinity.

"Luken described pre-infection as Stage 0. Infection was stage 1. The coma was stage 2. And the final stage – stage 3 – was where Kari was no longer human.

"I will not go into the details of how this virus works on all its levels. I am only concerned with telling you its ultimate purpose. Like any virus, it is to self-replicate, and it accomplishes this by directing the host to attack all living things in sight. Live specimens were given to Kari, to feed upon. She ate them alive, and only grew stronger. Her biomass increased – not just her weight, but her skeletal structure, her muscles, her hunger.

"Eventually, it became too much. She was able to use her strength to break free from her cell. They should have killed her while they had the chance."

I hadn't said a word up to this point. It was hard not to be sick at what I heard.

"So that...thing..." Makara shook her head. "It's still alive?"

Samuel nodded. "Yes, very much so. I don't know exactly where she is. But she is most likely by the elevators. After all, that is probably where all the people ran."

I tried not to focus on the picture that popped into my mind – Kari, gnawing on human flesh and bone in the darkness.

"But...how are we supposed to get out?" I asked. "Surely there must be a way."

"There are only two ways," Samuel said. "One is the tunnel, but the exit is surrounded by the sleeping spores. There is only one gas mask. And it is not as if that area is safe, either; after all, I had come in that way on my return to Bunker 114, only to be ambushed by Kari. Of the six men, I was the only one who survived."

"Wouldn't the elevators be worse, though?" I asked.

"The elevators are our only option. We will have to climb up the shaft and take one of the vehicles out."

"Vehicles?" Makara asked.

Samuel nodded. "There are several Recons in the motor pool near the top of the mountain. We could use one of those. They run on hydrogen and are all-terrain."

Bunker 108 had a Recon, but it was hardly ever used because of the attention it would draw.

"Look," I said, "a Recon sounds fine and all, but it will be of no use if we're all dead. What about those gas masks your patrol was wearing? I could go out, get them, and bring them back for everyone to use. Wouldn't it be safer to get into the motor pool from the outside?"

"It is impossible to reach if from outside. Everything is locked tight, and it's a long way to walk. I wish it were that easy. I have another reason why we need to exit by the elevator."

"That's obvious," Makara said. "Free Recons. If we could each grab one, we'd be rich."

"I have another purpose in mind," Samuel said.

"Of course you do," Makara said, sitting back.

"While researching the xenovirus, I discovered a curious citation in the databanks, by a certain Dr. Cornelius Ashton."

Makara looked up. "Cornelius Ashton? That name sounds familiar for some reason."

"Because he lived and researched at Bunker One. He is the author of a research paper called the Black Files."

My ears perked at that. "The Black Files...I've heard my dad talk about them. He'd wanted to get his hands on those for years."

Samuel nodded. "The Black Files contain a wealth of information about the xenovirus that was lost when Bunker One fell. No one thought to save the data and transport it back west." Samuel sighed. "To think of all that information...there may even be something about a cure, or how to stop Blights from growing..."

"How do you know if such information might be in the Files?" Makara asked. "Sounds like wishful thinking to me."

"I don't know," Samuel said. "Dr. Luken, and Dr. Keener, both certainly seemed to think they held something. The way Dr. Luken describes it in his notes..." Samuel shook his head. "Though much of our knowledge of the xenovirus comes from the Black Files, no one I know has ever actually *read* them. Think about it, Makara: the xenovirus was in a higher state of evolution while we were living in Bunker One in Colorado, than it is here now in California. With their personnel and resources, Bunker One would have an amazing amount of research."

Makara and I looked at each other. I had no idea what any of this meant, and why it meant we had to sneak past Kari, climb up a long elevator shaft in the darkness, and commandeer a Recon.

"Samuel," Makara said. "What are you saying?"

"Think about it," Samuel said. "We may finally know the origins of the xenovirus. Where it came from. How to stop it. Answers we cannot find here."

"Oh no," Makara said. "Samuel..."

"Don't tell me..." I said.

Samuel looked at Makara, then me.

"We have to go back," Samuel said. "We have to find Bunker One."

Chapter 21

No one said anything for a long while.

Then, Makara spoke. "What do you mean, 'go back'? You do realize Bunker One is nearly one thousand miles from here? Even with a Recon, that's a lot of open terrain to cover. And winter is coming on. How do we even find..."

"I'm not pretending to know all the answers," Samuel said. "I really do believe that the xenovirus could take over the world. The Blights have grown for all our whole lives with no sign of abatement. I fear that it could engulf the entire planet if no one does anything."

"So," I said, "we're the heroes, now?"

"I can't do this alone, Alex," Samuel said. "If not us, who will?"

I paused. I just wanted to be in a town with plenty of food and safety. I was tired of this running around. But this xenovirus had already ended both Bunkers in California. We were down to two, now, and I didn't even know where those were.

How long before entire towns were leveled? And who in the world, besides us, knew about the true threat the xenovirus posed? Both research facilities were gone, now. Maybe they had been the only two left in the world.

"This...could be nothing," Makara said. "Do you really want to risk our lives traveling one thousand miles across the desert and mountains with winter coming on, especially when there is no guarantee that the Black Files will contain useful information? And, need I remind you, at the time of year when raiders are returning to Bluff?"

"Yes. We have to take that chance, because no one else will."

Makara folded her arms and scowled. She didn't like this, and I didn't blame her. I wasn't sure I liked it, either. But I could see Samuel's point. If we could find a cure for this thing, wouldn't it be worth all that trouble?

Makara cast me a worried look. I wondered what she was thinking.

"Return with us to Oasis, Samuel," Makara said. "We can wait out the worst of the winter behind walls. Then, when spring comes, we can go."

Samuel frowned. He did not like that idea.

"That takes too much time," he said. "Besides, Ohlan is a weasel and I do not trust him."

"No argument there," I said.

"So, what do we do?" Makara asked.

"If neither of you can go," Samuel said, "then you may return to Oasis. I will head to Cheyenne alone."

Makara shook her head. "No."

A thousand questions crossed my mind. Was I going to Colorado? How would we find it? Where would we find food? How would we survive the winter? How would we even escape Bunker 114?

"First, let's talk about getting out of here," I said. "The rest is details if we end up dying in this place."

"I agree," Samuel said. "Sometimes, I think too far ahead."

Makara leaned forward. "So, how do we get to the motor pool?"

"We have to leave this section of the Bunker," Samuel said. "Travel the corridors, until we reach the elevators. They're located in the power plant. Large reactors take up the entire floor, and there's a bridge we can take over them. Obviously, the elevators won't work, but we can climb the shaft until we reach the Nest, near the peak of Cold Mountain. The Nest was actually the main entrance to Bunker 114 when the first refugees came in, but the area has been closed off now for a long time. However, the motor pool is there. There is access to a mountain road that, with luck, will not be buried by rock, sand, and snow. Even so, the Recon should handle it."

"How do we know the Recons still work?" Makara asked.

"They're too valuable an asset for 114 to have let them fall in disrepair. They will be running fine."

"I hope so," Makara said.

"The only part that worries me is getting past Kari," Samuel said.

I gave a short laugh. "At least you're just worried. It kind of takes my 'absolutely terrified' down a notch."

"Seriously," Makara said. "How do we get past a monster that leveled an entire Bunker?"

"The best idea is not to fight," Samuel said. "Infected creatures, whatever they are, only move when given a reason. Loud noises will only attract more of them."

"And just how do we kill something that big without guns?" Makara asked.

"If it comes down to it, we'll shoot," Samuel said. "They fall just like we do. They might have a great deal more pain tolerance. A sure way is to go for the head."

"So if we have to fight this thing," I said. "Aim for the head?"

Samuel nodded. "If we do this right, we shouldn't have to even fight. All the same, it pays to be prepared.

"What else do I need to know?" I asked.

"Nothing. Just follow my lead. Thankfully, we're in the dorms, so there will be plenty of supplies – everything we will need in the future. Warm clothing, food, and spare ammunition are a must. Colorado is a long way, and I don't mean to die on the journey."

"Good," Makara said. "Let's suit up, then."

***

Samuel returned us our old packs. I'd almost forgotten about them. All that ammunition, and of course the batts, would be useful later.

We went through the rooms, Makara listing all the things we would need on the road: cold weather gear, food, extra weapons. In the dorms there were plenty of clothes. I found a heavy desert camo jacket, a beanie, gloves, and thermal underwear. If it was already this cold, it was hard to imagine what winter would be like in a couple months.

Whatever room was left over we filled with food and ammunition. I carried the food, Makara the ammunition. Samuel had miscellaneous supplies: a handheld radio, a lighter, a small stove, among other things we would need upside. He easily carried the most of all of us, but he was also the strongest.

I found myself a long, serrated combat knife. It attached right on my belt, opposite of my Beretta. I also grabbed a few extra boxes of 9mm rounds.

All packed, we met in front of the vault door that was the entrance to the dormitories. Everything felt heavy on my shoulders.

"Alright," Samuel said. "I'm opening the door."

I felt a chill pass over me. When Makara got out her knife, I took mine out also.

I held my breath as Samuel turned the wheel that would unlock the door. Makara's face was calm, ready. I wondered how she could be so cool and collected.

The door creaked open, echoing in the outside corridor. Unlike where we stood, where it was light and ordered, the outside was dark and chaotic. Loose papers, broken electronics, and snapped lines all littered the corridor. Blood stained the walls and streaked the floors. A rotten musk hung in the air. Ahead of us, the corridor angled ninety degrees to the right. A painted, yellow arrow pointed, saying "Exit."

"Follow me," Samuel said. "And stay quiet."

Samuel walked out, and we followed him.

We rounded the corner, and Makara's flashlight clicked on. It looked like we were at the scene of a grisly murder. There was blood everywhere – the walls, the floor, the doors. It was as if the creature had consciously painted everything red to mark its territory. In the corners grew tufts of pink fungus.

It was quiet, and cold. There was a deadening of sound, and our footsteps did not echo but stopped at the walls.

We were walking for several minutes when we came to an intersection. A rush of cold wind blew through the deserted corridor. From where it came, I could not tell. But it was not natural.

Samuel held his hand up, indicating us to hang back. We did so, and he crept up to the crossroads. He stood in the middle of it for a moment. Then something massive rushed past in a blur. It snatched Samuel as it scuttled past on multiple legs. Samuel grunted, and was gone from sight.

"Samuel!" Makara yelled.

She ran into the darkness. I was right behind her. We turned in the direction Samuel had been taken.

But the hallway was empty.

I pointed to the floor. A trail of a clear liquid led from where we stood to an open doorway on our right. It looked like he had been dragged in.

Makara ran, and I followed her. I held my gun in front of me.

We had entered a common area. A pool table sat in front of us, and a large television screen, shattered, sat in the corner. Makara shot the flashlight beam around the room.

The wind blew again, chilling me to the bone. I spun around, but there was nothing but darkness.

"This way," Makara said.

I followed Makara across glass spread across the floor. It crunched under our boots. The walls were colored pink with fungus. In a far, dark corner of the room, I could see the outlines of the couch. And on the couch, a body.

Makara and I ran up to it. It was Samuel, his body was wrapped in a thin, white coating of...something.

Samuel!" Makara hissed.

"What happened?" I asked. "Where is that thing?"

Samuel stared past us, at the ceiling. The floor below us darkened. I felt the cold wind, close, tickling the back of my neck from above.

I looked up to see an enormous spider.

Makara screamed.

As I aimed my Beretta, the thing opened its mouth, revealing a long stinger that was curved and bladelike. From the end, poison dripped. It screeched as it swiped it at me. I dodged just in time.

At the same time, a hairy, muscular leg clobbered me. The force was so great that I fell and rolled to the other side of the room, where I hit the wall.

I struggled to get up. The arachnid was huge, standing on eight legs, each one the height of a person. It was covered with sticky, pink flesh. A pool of slime collected beneath its body, dripping from its mouth, its fangs, its many white eyes. Two large, serrated pincers opened and closed, longing for a taste of either of us. And the blade, set inside its mouth, was cruel and pointed, flexing back and forth.

With me out of the way, the creature knocked Makara to the ground. It moved over her, its fangs opening, sharp blade arching back.

I got up, doing my best to hold my gun steady. I started shooting.

Bam. Bam. Bam.

The shots reverberated in the room, deafening me. The creature squealed. I had hit it on its side, but it hardly made a dent – purple liquid oozed out, running down its leg. It shook itself, and then turned to face me. It scuttled toward me, its pincers chomping open and closed.

I shot again, hitting it in an eye. It screamed in pain – on its breath I could smell the rot of other victims. Still, it crawled closer, just feet away.

I shot, over and over, right into its face. When it opened its pincers, I could see inside its mouth. I shot it there.

The spider went rigid. I jumped out of the way and continued to shoot, aiming at the head. The hideous creature crawled on its belly toward me. Finally, the magazine was empty. I wouldn't even have time to switch it out. The thing was only feet away.

I got out my knife, stabbing into the thing's head, over and over. It shuddered, then lay down on the ground, dead. I retrieved my knife. It was coated in pink slime.

I wiped it on some nearby furniture and ran to Makara, who was lying on the floor. I knelt beside her, and shook her by the shoulders.

"Makara! Makara!"

Her eyes opened.

I looked all over her body, but could see no wound.

"Can you stand?"

"I'm...I'm fine. I just...do not care for spiders."

She began to sit up, and crawled to the couch where Samuel was. I helped her over to him.

"Makara," he said.

"Samuel, you idiot, why did you go ahead? What were you thinking?"

Samuel shook his head. "I'm sorry. I saw something and didn't want to risk everyone." He struggled to move. "Can you get me out of this damn thing?"

"What is it?" I asked.

"Spider silk," Makara said. "Luckily it isn't too thick. It shouldn't take long to pull off."

For the next few minutes, we cut and tore at the spider thread. Soon, Samuel burst out and stood next to us, and began to pull the icky stuff off his clothes.

"I'm glad it didn't bite me," he said. "I would have been toast. I would have never imagined such a thing could grow to that size."

"What else is in this place?" Makara asked.

"I don't know, but we're not staying to find out," Samuel said. "Kari is still somewhere in here. We're leaving."

Chapter 22

Before leaving the room, I switched out my Beretta's magazine. I had a feeling I would be using it before long.

"Go left here," Samuel said.

We turned. This entire side of the Bunker had been completely taken over by the xenovirus. The floor was carpeted in pink and purple fungus and strange stalactites hung from the ceiling, dripping slimy liquid. We did our best to avoid them.

We turned into a long hallway, and my breath caught. We were in a gigantic chamber, standing on a metal bridge spanning darkness. Below, I could see shapes of large machines, now dark and defunct. These had been the nuclear reactors that had once powered the entire Bunker. They were offline, now – the dorms must have been running on a backup source of power. Above, two large streams of sunlight spilled in from holes in the high ceiling, casting spotlights on the floor below.

Across the bridge, I could see three sets of metal doors.

"The elevators are ahead," Samuel said.

We started across the bridge, our footfalls echoing hard off the metal.

We were a third of the way across when a massive shape sailed through the air from one of the machines. It pummeled into the bridge right in front of us.

It was a giant humanoid, probably three times the height of a person. Sickly, pink flesh covered its entire body without a trace of hair. Long claws extended from its massive hands. Its eyes were narrow slits, white and glowing. Muscles bulged under sinewy skin, ready to inflict destruction. Bloody gashes, dripping purple goo, lashed up and down its body. Its reek made me feel like a tsunami of raw sewage was washing over me.

A low rumble sounded from its throat.

"Kari," Samuel said.

Kari charged. Makara lifted her gun and fired, six times, but only hitting the monster's muscular chest. All of them entered, but did nothing to slow her. Samuel also gave a few shots, but only managed to hit Kari's shoulder.

I aimed my gun for the head.

Bam. Bam.

I missed twice. She was near, and took a swipe for my gun. It clattered to the grated metal floor and slid away, almost falling off the edge.

Makara worked to reload, but the beast had turned on her. Makara pulled out her knife and took a swing, her face grim. She made two deep slashes on Kari's abdomen. The creature screamed, and slammed against Makara. Makara banged against the handrail, wincing in pain.

I got on the floor to get my gun. But somehow, Kari saw me. As she turned to go after me, Makara stabbed her in the leg.

Kari howled, the thick muscles under her thin skin flexing. Purple slime surged from her wounds. She swung her right arm in a wide arc, pummeling Makara on the shoulder. Makara dropped her gun, the force of the blow knocking her hard against the railing – so hard, that she was being pushed over the edge of it.

This time, she was going to fall.

"No!"

I ran forward, but Samuel got there first. He grabbed Makara's hands, pulling her back. Kari roared, standing high on her legs. She raised her right arm, readying a swipe to end them both.

I charged, going for Kari's giant legs. My shoulder met the mass of flesh and muscle. On contact, Kari's knees buckled and her knees slammed onto the bridge.

From both sides of the chasm, I could hear a foreboding creak.

"The bridge is going to fall!" I said.

Makara and I grabbed Samuel, running for the elevators.

We ran as fast as we could, Samuel loping along. Then, he started running, too, outpacing the both of us.

Then, the bridge began to fall. Samuel and Makara reached the landing in front of the elevators, but I felt the bridge falling from under me. Kari was just steps behind. Then, I jumped, sailing through the air. Makara reached out for me. Samuel grabbed Makara from the back. When I landed in Makara's arms, she held on tight. We were both anchored by Samuel lying on the ground, pushing his legs against one of the bridge posts.

Behind, I could hear Kari let out a horrible shriek that echoed throughout the chamber. I turned to see her flailing on the bridge, getting twisted in it. Then, there was a massive crash as the bridge hit the bottom floor.

We lay there for a while, catching our breaths. I couldn't believe we were still alive.

Samuel stood, and walked toward the edge of the platform.

"She is at peace, now," he said.

Samuel walked past us, to the elevator doors. With his powerful arms and shoulders, he forced them open. He went inside, and reached for the ceiling, opening the escape hatch.

After all we had been through, especially after surviving Kari, climbing the elevator shaft was easy. We took frequent breaks. I don't know how high it was, but we were climbing the ladder for at least thirty minutes.

By the time we reached the top, I was sore. Samuel, from the top, was able to use his strength to push the doors open.

I was the last one up, and when I walked through the doors, I was met with a foyer lined with dust. The room was circular in shape, and a long, wide corridor sloping upward led out.

Makara shined her flashlight ahead.

"This is the Nest," Samuel said. "The motor pool will be by the front entrance."

The place, besides the dust, was surprisingly clean. Samuel was right; no one had been here in a long, long time. However, there was a thin trail running through the dust that led to a heavy side door. Some people had come through here.

"That's the way in," Samuel said. "Just a few minutes more, and we'll be out of here."

We were now in the front entry hall. I imagined what it must have been like, all those thirty years ago, when the panicked refugees had filed in; to go down those elevators, and never come back up.

We now stood in front of the door. There was a keycard slot next to it, but when Samuel tried the door, it opened right up.

We stepped into the motor pool. It was so dark that it was all Makara's flashlight could do to illumine the place. The place smelled of oil and machinery. It reminded me of our own motor pool at Bunker 108.

Then, we saw them. There were three Recons, all lined up and facing outward toward large, pull-up garage doors. They each had four wheels with thick, serrated all-terrain tires, with plenty of suspension to hold up the chassis. Each one was a light brown desert camo, and the cabs were thin and aerodynamic, hanging low to the ground. These things were built for speed. There looked to be enough room for four people in each. In the back was a large turret, upon which was mounted a machine gun. Its height meant that it probably had 360 degree rotation, and it would have no problem shooting over the cab. In the back, below the machine gun, was a sizeable space for cargo. The hydrogen fuel tank would be in there, right behind the cab.

"Wicked," I said.

"Let's check them out," Samuel said.

We inspected all three. Each had a cargo bay in the back, filled with spare parts, a couple of spare tires, tools, and even some rations and water. We gathered all we could into the center Recon. I went to the passenger door, finding it locked.

"Needs a key," I said.

"They're over here, on the wall," Samuel said, taking one down. "This one should do it."

I held out my hands. Instead of tossing it to me, he handed it off to Makara.

"Hey," I said.

"You don't know how to drive," Makara said.

"And you do?"

"It's been a while...but yeah. The Lost Angels had a Recon, so I know how to pilot it."

"I want to learn."

"Maybe later." Makara put an index finger to her chin. "She needs a name."

Everyone stopped, and thought a moment.

"We'll think of something later," Samuel said. "A good name is important. We have to get it right."

Makara nodded. "You're right. Have we got everything?"

"I think so," Samuel said. "Fire her up. Alex, help me with the garage door."

Makara opened the driver's door and hopped in. The Recon started with a roar that faded into a low hum. The hum came from behind the cab, where the hydrogen fuel tank was building pressure.

Samuel and I unlatched the garage door, pulling it up to reveal the outside. Light flooded the garage, blinding me for a moment. The cold mountain air rushed in, stinging my face with cold.

When my eyes adjusted, I was startled to see the sky above, not a dull red, but a blue violet. We were above the low hanging clouds.

Right above, I saw the sun for the first time in my life.

I didn't have time to enjoy it, though. Samuel hit me on the shoulder. He pointed down the disused road curving down the mountain through rock and red-tinged snow. My eyes narrowed.

Walking up the path were five men, maybe two hundred yards away. They stopped, clearly seeing us.

"Inside the Recon," Samuel said. "Now."

We ran into the garage as the first shots fired.

I had no idea how, but Brux had found us.

Chapter 23

We piled in the Recon. Makara turned on us.

"What the hell are they doing here?"

"I don't know," I said. "Just drive!"

Makara shifted into drive and floored it. The engine roared and the pressure tank behind us hummed. The tires squealed on the pavement as the Recon roared onto the dirt road covered with snow.

"Careful," Samuel said. "This road is narrow."

"They're straight ahead," I said. "Makara, I don't think you should..."

"Get down," she said.

The raiders opened fire on us. I heard bullets ding off the hood and hit the windshield. Three bullets cracked the glass.

"Here we go," she said.

I heard men yelling from the sides of the vehicle, but no tell-tale squishy bumps.

The guns fired a few more times, but we were in the clear. We sped past them.

"Next stop, Bunker One," Makara said.

"Makara," I said, "don't ever try that again."

She cracked a smile. "It worked, didn't it?"

"Yeah, but you could've been shot."

She shrugged. "Are you really complaining here?"

I sighed. "I guess you have a point."

We rounded a bend. Below I could see red clouds spread out like a blanket over the land, and mountaintops poking through them. We would be entering those clouds soon. Already, they were closer.

A few minutes later, we were in the dense, red fog. Makara turned on the headlights, but we could only see a few yards in front of us.

"I don't see how they found us," I said.

"Maybe they weren't trying," Makara said. "They're hurting for loot to take back. Now that Bunker 114 is gone, maybe they thought it would be easy pickings." She shook her head. "Idiots."

Makara slowed down. The entire right side was sheer cliff, and falling off would mean death.

It was after we had gone down several switchbacks that I noticed two pairs of headlights above us.

"Shit," I said. "They followed us!"

I couldn't believe I'd forgotten about those other two vehicles. Of course this wasn't over yet.

"I'm afraid you will have to drive fast now, Makara," Samuel said. "I'm going in the back to man the turret."

"Get back there, then," Makara said. "Be careful."

Samuel disappeared into the back. A few seconds later, he had started firing.

A spray of bullets showered the road ahead of us from above. We took a tight turn, forcing everyone to the left. The entire Recon shook with the effort.

I got out my Beretta, not knowing what good it would do me in this vehicle. The other Recons were two switchbacks above us.

"Can't we go faster?" I asked.

Makara's look was venomous. "If you want to slip on the ice and snow and fall to our deaths, then yeah...we can go faster."

"Good point."

Then, the first Recon rounded the bend right behind us. Samuel fired. I could see the hood of the other vehicle become riddled with bullets. A raider leaned out the passenger's window and fired toward us.

Makara swerved around a tight bend, and the back tires lost traction. We were heading toward the cliff. At the last moment, Makara floored it, and we were surging ahead onto the next downward slope. I thought my heart was going to beat out of my chest.

The next Recon tried the same thing, only it was going too fast. As it fishtailed, the back tires fell off the slope. The entire vehicle slid backward, its front tires squealing like some dying thing.

As we rounded the next bend, we could see the Recon toppling over the road ahead of us.

Makara slammed on the brakes as Samuel fired a hail of bullets at the other Recon, just one switchback above us. The downed Recon crashed into the road ahead, did a half flip, and continued to roll down the mountainside.

"They're done," I said.

A moment later, the vehicle exploded in a violent plume of fire, crashing into a giant rock jutting out from the mountain.

"Let's hope Brux was in there," Makara said.

That was not to be. The other Recon swerved around the corner. In the passenger's seat, I could see the man with the blonde crew cut and a long scar, even from the side mirror. The driver's eyes were wide and fearful. Brux looked murderous.

We exited the layer of red fog, finding ourselves very close to the desert floor. The snow petered out, replaced by red rock, dirt, and barren Waste. We made one final turn, and it was a straight stretch to the desert flatland.

Then, I heard a popping noise. I turned, and the low hum of the pressure chamber became a high whir. The pressure needle on the fuel gauge swerved down.

"They must have hit something," Makara said. "We're losing pressure."

"What does that mean?

"It means we're going nowhere."

Behind us, after another round of shooting, I heard the tires of Brux's Recon squeal. Samuel had blown out one of the tires. The vehicle swerved, and flipped on its side. It slid down the hill, past us, even as our Recon slowed to a halt and the electronics powered down.

Makara braked, bringing our Recon to a halt. She hopped out of the vehicle, pointing her pistol at Brux's vehicle, the bottom of which now faced us.

I got out on my side, and followed Makara's example, pointing my gun at the raiders' crashed vehicle. Samuel faced the turret toward the downed Recon.

It was time to meet Brux.

Chapter 24

Nothing happened for a full minute. We just stood there, pointing our guns, waiting for anyone to come out. The wind blew, blowing dust across the scene.

After waiting a while, I was beginning to think they might be dead.

But quick as a flash, Brux showed himself and fired a few shots. Above us, we heard Samuel give a loud yell.

Brux slipped behind the downed Recon, a smile on his lips.

"Samuel!" Makara said.

Samuel grabbed his shoulder and dropped inside the cargo bay. Makara and I jumped inside. He was sitting in the corner next to some supplies, holding his right shoulder and grimacing.

"Oh my God," Makara said.

She ripped down the first aid kit hanging on the wall.

Samuel winced. "Pressure...put pressure on the wound..."

Makara ripped open her bag, taking out a shirt. She placed it on the wound, where blood gushed out at an alarming rate. Makara put her full weight on it. Samuel groaned.

"Alex, find the congealing agent," she said.

I opened the first aid kid, digging through it. I found a tube of liquid that had the word "congealer" on it.

"This it?"

Makara snatched it from me. She took off the shirt, and squeezed the clear jelly onto the wound. Samuel hissed with pain. She put pressure back on the wound.

"That should help," she said.

Samuel waved her away. "It's nothing. Let me hold the shirt."

"Samuel, you're in no state..."

He pushed her off with surprising strength, holding the shirt. "I will be fine for the next few minutes. You have to deal with Brux."

Makara nodded. "You're right. But, how?"

I was afraid to step out of the cargo bay. Surely, their sights would be trained on the back, the only exit. Stepping out there was sure death.

"I have an idea," I said.

Both Makara and Samuel looked at me.

"The pressure tank...has it lost all pressure?"

"No," Samuel said. "There should be some fuel left."

"Don't strain yourself, Samuel." She turned to me. "Alex, what's your idea?"

"Hydrogen." I tapped the tank. "There's still plenty of it in reserve. If we can take the tank and throw it out the back, it will roll down the hill. If one of us shoots it..."

Samuel smiled. "Boom."

"But how will we get away without our own pressure tank?" Makara asked.

"We can salvage the tank off the other Recon afterward."

"If it doesn't blow up in the process," Makara said.

"That's a risk we'll have to take," I said. "This is our only option."

Makara nodded. "Let's do it."

Getting it out was easy – the pressure tanks were meant to be easily installed and removed. The thing was heavy. It took both me and Makara lifting it to get it to the back of the Recon.

We looked at each other.

"Ready?" I asked.

Makara nodded. "Let's hope this works."

We tossed it out, making sure it was horizontal to the slope. We gave a few seconds for the thing to roll down the hill.

"Now," I said.

Makara stepped out the back, and started to fire. I jumped onto the turret, and didn't bother with the heavy gun. I aimed my Beretta toward the tank.

They were hiding. We met no resistance as I opened fire.

My bullets connected, and the tank lit up like a torch. A giant mushroom of fire shot upward, forcing the downed Recon backward, causing it to roll on its top.

I jumped down from the turret as Makara joined me. I took out my handgun. It was time to finish the job.

As we wheeled around the vehicle, we found both Brux and his crony lying on the ground. The crony lifted a pistol. I shot him dead before he had the chance to fire. He went limp, and relaxed against the earth.

Brux was a few feet off, his skin cracked and charred. His entire body was shaking. He reached for his gun, just a few feet off. Makara kicked it far away.

"Ma...Makara..." Brux said, lifting an arm in surrender.

Behind us, the fire of our improvised bomb still crackled. It was nowhere near this Recon's hydrogen tank, so were safe for now.

Makara walked by his head, pointing her gun down. "Don't try anything, Brux. You've had your time to try."

"I...I won't. Please...have mercy on me, Makara. I'm sorry. Take me back to Bluff...I'll give you money, anything you want."

Makara scowled as her eyes considered. Surely, she couldn't be...

Bam.

The bullet went right into Brux's forehead. His entire body stiffened, then was still. His vacant eyes stared upward.

The wind blew cold as Makara spat on his face.

"Come on," she said. "We need to rescue that other tank."

I followed Makara into the upside down Recon. Thankfully, the cargo bay had been left wide open. Together, we removed the tank. Hydrogen gas hissed into the air from the fuel line. It would only be moments before it connected with the flames not too far away.

"Let's get out of here," Makara said.

We jumped out of the Recon and ran back uphill, lugging the tank with us. As we reached our own vehicle, the downed Recon ignited, booming off the nearby mountainside. I could feel its heat licking at my back.

We went back into the cargo bay. While Makara installed the new tank and connected it to the fuel line, I made sure Samuel was alright. The bleeding had slowed, but his face was pale. If he did not get medical attention soon, the bullet would eventually take his life.

Makara finished making the connections, and nodded. She put a hand on Samuel's shoulder.

Samuel forced a smile. "It's nothing."

"Humph." She looked toward me. "Let's get him up front."

Makara and I moved him to the passenger's seat. As Makara slid to the driver's side, I sat in the middle.

"You're in charge of watching him," Makara said. "Let's hope she starts up."

Makara turned the key, and the engine roared to life. As soon as I heard the engine idle, and the pressure tank hum, I knew what her name would be.

"Khloe," I said.

Makara raised an eyebrow. "Khloe? That's not a tough name for a Recon."

"You're wrong. It's the toughest name I know."

She looked at me for a moment, and then nodded. "Khloe it is, then."

Samuel's eyes closed as Makara drove Khloe east. In the side mirror, I could see the fires of the downed Recon burn brightly.

We sped across the flat Wasteland, Cold Mountain a mass behind us.

On our left, I could see a couple of infected wolves feeding on the body of a fallen antelope. As we passed, they sped after us, oblivious of any danger to themselves. We quickly left them in our dust.

I shook my head. "The first normal animal I see ends up being eaten by some infected wolves. Figures."

From beside us, Samuel was still.

"Is he alright?" I asked.

Makara watched him for a moment. "Let him rest. He will need it."

"He needs medical attention."

"You think I don't know that? We will be there by tonight."

"Where?"

"You're not going to like it."

"Oh no. Not Oasis."

"Guess again."

I thought about it, but nothing came to mind. Surely not L.A.. That was too far. But where else could she...

Then, Samuel spoke, his voice raspy.

"Don't tell me we're going to Raider Bluff, little sister."

Makara smiled grimly. "It's the homecoming we've all been waiting for. I have a favor to call in."

"What?" I asked. "You're not serious..."

"It's the only place I know with a doctor," Makara said. "I don't like it, but it's the only option."

The cab was quiet for a moment. Finally, Samuel gave a long, tired sigh.

"Lead on, then."

I thought we were out of the fire, but now, we were going into the furnace. Makara stepped on the gas, as if to defiantly meet that inevitability.

We surged ahead. As I watched the Wasteland pass, even as we made enormous speed, Cheyenne Mountain and Bunker One had never seemed more far away.

About the Author

Kyle West is a science fiction author living in Oklahoma City. He is currently working on *The Wasteland Chronicles* series, of which there will be seven installments. The next two books, *Origins* and *Evolution*, are already available. To find out immediately when the next book is released, sign up for The Wasteland Chronicles Mailing List, found at eepurl.com/A1-8D.

Origins Preview

Samuel was dying.

We had left Bunker 114 and Cold Mountain behind hours ago and darkness cloaked the Wasteland. As we sped east toward Raider Bluff, I wondered if Brux's parting shot meant our mission had failed before it even began.

Samuel's eyes had remained closed for almost the entire journey. Wet blood soaked his right shoulder. The congealing agent had slowed the bleeding somewhat, but he wouldn't last for long. We had to find someone who could remove the bullet and stop the bleeding. If we couldn't, either Makara or I would have to do it.

The Recon's bright blue lights pushed back the night, letting us to see ahead in a wide arc. Thirty years of red dust covered most parts of the highway. We zoomed past decrepit buildings, ghost towns, and mangled road signs, the skeletal remains of Ragnarok.

Makara was going as fast as the heavy Recon would go – about fifty five miles per hour, the wheels churning to get us to our destination.

I just didn't know if it was fast enough.

When the highway turned south, I could see on our left a wide dark river, flowing south.

"We hit the Colorado," Makara said.

It was more water than I'd ever seen in my life. I'd read about the Colorado River in the Bunker 108 archive. It had once been an important river in the Old World, but overuse had dried it up. Now, the river was wide, so wide, in fact, that I couldn't see the other side in the darkness. Above the river on the opposite bank, high up, I could see the city. Raider Bluff's yellow lights glowed dimly with distance, almost unmoving even with the Recon's speed.

At last, the road turned left, toward the river. I could see a bridge of tall arches spanning the water.

"Silver Arched Bridge," Makara said. "The only crossing for miles."

The giant rungs of the arch stretched from shore to shore with the road running straight underneath. The road itself was almost even with the river - maybe just ten feet above it. The pressure from the current must be enormous. Two raiders with rifles guarded the bridge's front.

"Let me do the talking," Makara said.

We pulled up, and Makara rolled down her window.

A hard-faced, grizzled man peered inside. His eyes widened upon seeing who was driving.

"Makara?"

"Chris, step aside. I have a wounded man in here who will die without medical attention."

"What?" Chris asked. He shined the flashlight inside the Recon, pointing the beam at Makara, Samuel, and then me. "What happened? Where's Brux? Jade? Tyson?"

"All dead. Let me through, and I don't have time for these questions!"

"What happened?"

"Gunshot wound," Makara said. "Now step aside unless you want me to run you over!"

"Not so fast," he said. "I'm not putting my ass on the line until you answer some questions. First, who is this?" he asked, pointing at me.

"Look, Chris," Makara said, "Just give me clearance to Char or I'll have him wipe the floor with you. I promise, you not listening to me is more dangerous than this sixteen-year-old kid and a man dying from a gunshot wound."

Chris sighed, his gaze doing its best to match up with Makara's. But after a moment, he turned away and raised his communicator to his mouth.

"Makara's back. I'm sending her up. Have the gates ready, over."

"Copy that, over," the voice said from the other end.

"Welcome home, Makara," Chris said, somewhat sarcastically. "You're clear. I hope you have a better story for Char than you do for me."

"I don't need a story, Chris." Makara said. "I need a doctor."

Makara was about to gun the accelerator when Chris grabbed her shoulder.

"What?" she asked, shrugging off his grasp.

"Be careful up there. Things have changed. An emissary from the Empire is in Bluff, talking with Char."

"The Empire?" Makara asked. "What the hell is the Empire?"

Chris frowned. "You were gone longer than I thought. They're based in Old Mexico. They're big, powerful – tens of thousands of people." He paused. "The emissary's name is Rex. Just don't get on his bad side. I know you can be mouthy."

Makara shook her head. "I'll say what I want, when I want, Chris. Is that it?"

"Yeah. You should head on. Just watch your back."

Makara didn't waste any more words on him. When Chris stepped aside, Makara floored the Recon, rocketing it into the night.

"The Empire," I said. "That sounds sinister."

"I've never heard of it before," Makara said. "Gone a few months, and this is what happens. The game always changes every time I come back. That's nothing new, though."

Despite those words, I could see the worry in her eyes.

"It's hard to imagine war at a time like this," I said. "The world is being taken over by the xenovirus. Leave it to humanity to take itself out first."

Makara sighed. "All the more reason to patch my brother up quickly and be on our way. We have a mission to finish."

I looked at Samuel. He was out again. Hopefully, it wasn't for good this time.

"Just a few minutes, Sam," Makara said. "Hang on."

***

We drove up what seemed an endless series of switchbacks before the land leveled and placed us before the wooden gates of Raider Bluff. These things were huge, probably three stories high. They made the gates of Oasis look like toys in comparison. A giant wooden palisade surrounded all sides of the town, maybe twenty feet high, as if the sheer cliffs weren't enough. It must have taken an eternity to build. I wondered where they found the labor, until I realized raiders were notorious for employing slaves.

At various points in the perimeter, large watchtowers rose. I had no idea where they had gotten the lumber to build these walls. Trees were growing *somewhere*, apparently, if not here. It was a testament to the citadel's wealth and power.

The gates then drew back, sliding into the walls on either side. Thick chains rigged to pulleys moved the massive fortifications. Even though I was about to enter the biggest den of thieves in all the world, I couldn't help but be impressed.

Makara drove down the main drag. Wooden buildings and saloons lined either side of the dirt road. It was like entering an Old West town on steroids. Signs swung above the open doors – liquor, girls, and guns seemed to be the establishments' main themes. Raiders dressed in dingy apparel flanked both sides of the road, making way for us as we came in. From their widened eyes, it was clear than none of them had seen a Recon before.

The raiders tried to get the Recon to stop but Makara honked the Recon's horn and sped up when they got too close.

"They're not going to hurt us," she said. "They just want to check out the ride."

Outside, I could hear them yelling her name.

"You seem to be pretty popular around here," I said.

"They're all idiots," Makara said.

The road wound its way around the mesa. I saw we were not even close to the top. There were three levels, and buildings rose from all of them. The bottom, which we were on now, was the largest. It seemed to contain all the places of business, the wide outdoor markets, the bars, pretty much anywhere you could buy something.

"We're heading to the Alpha's Compound," Makara said. "It's where Char lives. It's at the very top of Bluff and exclusive. No one will bother us, plus that's where the clinic is. Char, in addition to being the Alpha, is also good at stitching a wound. Hopefully this isn't beyond his expertise."

"Char was the one you raided with, right?"

Makara nodded. "Probably the only decent person who lives here. It's weird for a decent man to lead a bunch of scum. It's a wonder he's still alive."

We entered the second level. We were halfway up the bluff now. On either side were well-constructed wooden cabins.

Makara pointed out a small building we drove by. A sign overhung the door, reading, "The Bounty."

"That's the Bounty," Makara said. "It's a bar run by my friend Lisa. I've spent many-a-night there."

"I remember you mentioning it."

We rounded the last bend. Over the wooden rooftops of Bluff, I could see the vast panorama of dark desert. The black Colorado River flowed south and the sky above was dark and void.

We reached a final gate. A raider pulled it open from the other side, revealing a long cobblestone road that led into a grassy courtyard. The green grass must have been watered and cared for to flourish like that. Flanking either side of the road were tall pines. I rolled down my window, the trees' crisp, sweet smell pleasant yet foreign to my nostrils. I could see that the stone structure of the compound was a U-shape, surrounding the courtyard. It had narrow slits for windows; open air, no glass. Ahead, the cobblestone drive ended in a cul-de-sac. A wide, yet short, stairway led to a pair of heavy wooden doors. Judging from the thick stone walls, the compound had been constructed to withstand on all-out siege.

"Fancy," I said.

"It's grown over the last few years," Makara said. "Each new Alpha leaves his own mark. Char redid the courtyard. The pines were taken from mountains far to the east."

"Why is he called Char?" I asked.

Makara smiled grimly. "You will see."

Makara pulled to a stop in the cul-de-sac. She powered off the vehicle, the hum of the hydrogen pressure tank dimming to nothing.

We hopped out of the vehicle. The air was dry, cold, and sharp. It had definitely dropped a few degrees. We went to Samuel's side and opened the passenger's door. Makara and I lifted Samuel from the Recon.

He stirred a bit, and groaned. Though pale as a ghost, it was good to know he was still alive. Despite the sound he made, his whole body was limp. He was dead weight between us.

"Come on," Makara said. "We're going to have to drag him."

We dragged him through the compound, to the large front doors. Makara didn't bother knocking. She threw the doors open with her shoulder, revealing a wide, dark interior lit by torches. We dragged Samuel inside.

"Char!" Makara screamed.

Nothing answered her call. The entry hall was empty, lit only by two blazing braziers along the far wall and a few torches ensconced upon four heavy pillars supporting the room's structure.

Then, a shadow materialized in front of us, moving forward at lightning speed.

"Watch out!" I said.

Makara reached for her handgun with her free hand, never letting go of Samuel.

A thin, curved sword was placed at the base of Makara's neck.

"Not so fast," a young, female voice said.

***

Now standing in the light, the bearer of the sword was black-haired girl, about my age, with green almond eyes. The eyes narrowed as she edged the blade closer to Makara's throat. I saw that she was beautiful, with a short, yet curvy, figure. I berated myself for even noticing that at a time like this, but even at the threat of one's life, guys can't help but notice certain things.

"Who are you," she asked dangerously, "and what are you doing here?"

Makara spoke first, making an effort to keep calm. "We're here to see Char, girl. Put that thing away right now, or there's going to be trouble."

"Char is not here." The girl did not withdraw her sword. In fact, it looked like it was more in her mind to use it. "If you had been cleared, I would be the first to know. I'll give you one more chance. Tell me who you are, and why you're here. This wouldn't be the first assassination attempt I've stopped."

"I don't know who you think *you* are, but Char and I are old friends," Makara said, never batting an eyelash. "I'm Makara. Ever heard the name? And if you don't get us Char *right* now, then..."

The front doors banged open. I turned to see a grizzled man, probably in his fifties, enter.

"Makara," he said, his voice gravelly.

There was no mistaking the man's air of command. He was Char. He was tall with broad shoulders and a shaved head. Two guards flanked his either side, holding rifles. His sharp blue eyes surveyed us all calmly. He wore green camo pants and a thick black leather jacket. A tattoo of a snakelike dragon eating its own tail was emblazoned on his forearm. But his most striking feature was his face. A deep burn wound scarred his right cheek. That wound had happened long ago and would never fully heal.

No one said anything as the man stepped forward.

"I am sorry I was not here to greet you," he said to Makara. "Politics."

The girl glanced from Char to Makara, not sure what to do.

"Stand down, Anna," Char said. "I appreciate your drive to protect me, but Makara is a friend."

Anna pulled the blade back, sheathing it immediately. Those beautiful eyes stung with hurt. "Char, no one let me know of Makara's arrival."

"Your loyalty is admirable, but Makara is to be treated with the same respect you would afford any of my guests. More, in fact. But we don't have time to have hurt feelings, do we?"

He faced Samuel, who now lay on the ground between Makara and me.

"Lay him face-up," Char said. "I need to see the wound."

We set Samuel on the ground. Char walked forward and knelt beside him. He placed two fingers on his neck.

"There is a pulse," he said, his voice deep and gruff. Whatever had burned his face had also marred his voice. He glanced sideways at Makara. "Is the bullet still in?"

"Yes. It happened about ten hours ago."

"Humph."

Char retrieved a knife from his belt and cut Samuel's white tee shirt open at the shoulder. He pulled the fabric back tenderly to reveal the wound. Fresh red blood trickled out. The surrounding skin was black, purple, and green.

"He's out, now," Char said. "But he'll be dead if I try to pull it out of him like this. He needs morphine."

"You have that, don't you?" Makara asked.

Char grunted. "A bit. I do not want to use it on an outsider."

"My brother is not an outsider," Makara said. "He is family, as raider as anybody here."

"Don't worry," Char said. "I wouldn't let you bring him all this way to tell you no."

"Good. You had me worried." Makara eyes went up to Anna and narrowed, as if willing the katana-wielding girl away. Anna only stood, meeting Makara's stare without blinking.

"This is Anna, my bodyguard. You noticed her katana, I presume. She lives by the Bushido Code."

"Are you a samurai?" I asked.

Anna gave a single nod, but no word for answer.

Makara smirked. "I thought samurai were supposed to be Japanese. And men."

Judging from the look in Anna's eyes, she looked ready to draw her blade again.

"Honor and principle go beyond the confines of gender and race."

"She is deadly with a blade," Char said. "Where she learned to use it like that, I don't know. She's most of the reason why I've stayed Alpha so long. Especially these days. But all this is idle talk. Your brother needs my help." Char motioned to the raiders nearby. "We're taking Samuel to the clinic."

The men gathered around. Together, they lifted Samuel up.

"Follow me," Char said to Makara. Then, he noticed me for the first time. "Who's this?"

"Alex," I said.

"He's from Bunker 108," Makara said. "Once we take care of Samuel, we'll fill you in. It's a long, long story."

We followed Char and his bodyguards through the dark corridors and into the clinic.

Glossary

10,000, The: This refers to the 10,000 citizens who were selected in 2029 to enter Bunker One. This group included the best America had to offer, people who were masters in the fields of science, engineering, medicine, and security. President Garland and all the U.S. Congress, as well as essential staff and their families, were also chosen.

Alpha: "Alpha" is the title given to the recognized head of the raiders. In the beginning, it was only a titular role that only had as much power as the Alpha was able to enforce. But as Raider Bluff grew in size and complexity, the Alpha began to take on a more meaningful role. Typically, Alphas do not remain so for long – they are assassinated by rivals, who then rise to take their place. In some years, there can be as many as four Alphas – though powerful Alphas, like Char, can reign for many years.

Batts: Batts, or batteries, are the currency of the Wasteland. It is unknown *how* batteries were first seen as currency, but it is likely because they are small, portable, and durable. Rechargeable batteries are even more prized (called "chargers"), and solar batteries (called "solars," or "sols,") are the most useful and prized of all.

Black Files, The: The Black Files are the mysterious, collected research on the xenovirus, located in Bunker One. They were authored principally by Dr. Cornelius Ashton, Chief Scientist of Bunker One. Though Dr. Steven Keener believes in the Black Files existence, whether they are truly stored in Bunker One's archives is a matter of debate.

Black Reapers, The: The Black Reapers are a powerful, violent gang, based in Los Angeles. They are led by Warlord Carin Black. They keep thousands of slaves, using them to fuel their post-apocalyptic empire. They usurped the Lost Angels in 2055, and have been ruling there ever since.

Blights: Blights are infestations of xenofungus and the xenolife they support. They are typically small, but the bigger ones can cover large tracts of land. As a general rule of thumb, the larger the Blight, the more complicated and dangerous the ecosystem it maintains.

Bunker 108: Bunker 108 is located in the San Bernardino Mountains about one hundred miles east of Los Angeles. It is the birthplace of Alex Keener.

Bunker 114: A small, medical research installation built about fifty miles northwest of Bunker 108. Built beneath Cold Mountain, Bunker 114 is small. After the fall of Bunker One, Bunker 114, like Bunker 108 to the southeast, became a main center of xenoviral research.

Bunker One: The main headquarters of the Post-Ragnarok United States government. It fell in 2048 to a swarm of crawlers that overran its defenses. Bunker One had berths for ten thousand people, making it many times over the most populous Bunker. Its inhabitants included President Garland, the U.S. Senate and House of Representatives, essential government staff, security forces, along with the skilled people needed to maintain it. Also there were dozens of brilliant scientists and specialists, including engineers, doctors, and technicians. The very wealthy were also allowed berths for helping to finance the Bunker Program. Bunker One is also the location of the Black Files, authored by Dr. Cornelius Ashton.

Bunker Program, The: The United States and Canadian governments pooled resources to establish 144 Bunkers in Twelve Sectors throughout their territory. The Bunkers were the backup in case the Guardian Missions failed. When the Guardian Missions *did* fail, the Bunker Program kicked into full gear. The Bunkers were designed to save all critical government personnel and citizenry, along with anyone who could provide the finances to construct them. The Bunkers were designed to last indefinitely, using hydroponics to grow food. The Bunkers ran on fusion power, which had been made efficient by the early 2020's. The plan was, when the dust settled, Bunkers residents could reemerge and rebuild. Most Bunkers fell, however, for various reasons – including critical systems failures, mutinies, and attacks by outsiders (see **Wastelanders**). By the year 2060, only four bunkers were left.

Chaos Years, The: The Chaos years refers to the ten years following the impact of Ragnarok. These dark years signified the great die off of most forms of life, including humans. Most deaths occurred due to starvation. Crops could not grow in climates too far from the tropics due to mass global cooling. What crops *would* grow produced a yield far too paltry to feed the population that existed. This led to a period of violence unknown in all of human history. The Chaos Years signifies the complete breakdown of the Old World's remaining infrastructures – including food production, the economy, power grids, and industry, all of which led to the deaths of billions of people.

Dark Decade, The: The Dark Decade lasted from 2020-2030, from the time of first discovery of Ragnarok, to the time of its impact. It is not called the Dark Decade because the world descended into madness immediately upon the discovery of Ragnarok by astronomer Neil Weinstein – that only happened in 2028, with the failure of *Messiah*, the third and last of the Guardian Missions. In the United States and other industrialized nations, life proceeded in an almost normal fashion. There was plenty of hope and good reasons to believe that Ragnarok could be stopped, especially when given ten years. But as the Guardian Missions failed, one by one, the order of the world quickly disintegrated.

With the failure of the Guardian Mission, *Archangel*, in 2024, a series of wars engulfed the world. As what some were calling World

War III embroiled the planet, the U.S. and several of its European allies, and Canada, continued to work on stopping Ragnarok. When the second Guardian Mission, *Reckoning*, failed, an economic depression swept the world. But none of this compared to the madness that followed upon the failure of the third and final Guardian, *Messiah*, in 2028. As societies broke down, martial law was enforced. President Garland was appointed dictator of the United Sates with absolute authority. By 2029, several states had broken off from the Union.

In the last quarter of 2030, an odd silence hung over the world, as if it had grown weary of living. The President, all essential governmental staff and military, the Senate and House of Representatives, along with scientists, engineers, and the talented and the wealthy, entered the 144 Bunkers established by the Bunker Program. Outraged, the tens of millions of people who did not get an invitation found the Bunker locations, demanding to be let in. The military took action when necessary.

Then, on December 3, 2030, Ragnarok fell, crashing into the border of Wyoming and Nebraska, forming a crater one hundred miles wide. The world left the Dark Decade, and entered the Chaos Years.

Guardian Missions: The Guardian Missions were humanity's attempts to intercept and alter the course of Ragnarok during the Dark Decade. There were three, and in the order they were launched, they were called *Archangel*, *Reckoning*, and *Messiah* (all three of which were also the names of the ships launched). Each mission had a reason for failing. *Archangel* is reported to have crashed into Ragnarok, in 2024. In 2026, *Reckoning* somehow got off course, losing contact with Earth in the process. In 2028 *Messiah* successfully landed and attached its payload of rockets to the surface of Ragnarok in order to alter its course from Earth. However, the rockets failed before they had time to do their work. The failure of the Guardian Missions kicked the Bunker Program into overdrive.

Ice Lands, The: Frozen in a perpetual blanket of ice and snow, the northern and southern latitudes of the planet are completely unlivable. In the Wasteland at least, they are referred to as the Ice Lands. Under a blanket of meteor fallout, global cooling sent temperatures on Earth plummeting. While glaciers are only now experiencing rapid regrowth, they will advance for centuries, and perhaps millenniums, to come, until the fallout has dissipated enough to produce a warmer climate. In the Wasteland, 45 degrees north marks the beginning of what is considered the Ice Lands.

L.A. Gangland: L.A. Gangland means a much different thing than it did Pre-Ragnarok. In the ruins of Los Angeles, there are dozens of gangs vying for control, but by 2060, the most powerful is Black Reapers, who usurped that title from the Lost Angels.

Lost Angels, The: The Lost Angels were post-apocalyptic L.A.'s first super gang. From the year 2050 until 2055, they reigned supreme in the city, led by a charismatic figure named Dark Raine. The Angels were different from other gangs – they valued individual freedom and abhorred slavery. Under the Angels' rule, Los Angeles prospered. The Angels were eventually usurped in 2056 by a gang called the Black Reapers, led by a man named Carin Black.

Oasis: Oasis is a settlement located in the Wasteland, about halfway between Los Angeles and Raider Bluff. It has a population of one thousand, and is built around the banks of the oasis for which it is named. The oasis did not exist Pre-Ragnarok, but was formed by tapping an underground aquifer.

Raider Bluff: Raider Bluff is the only known settlement of the raiders. It is built northeast of what used to be Needles, California, across the Colorado River, on top of a three-tiered mesa. Though the raiders are mobile group, even they need a place to rest during the harsh, Wasteland winter. Merchants, women, and servants followed the raider men, setting up shop on the mesa, giving birth to Raider Bluff sometime in the early 2040's. From the top of the Bluff rules the Alpha, the strongest recognized leader of the raiders. A new Alpha rises only when he is able to wrest control from the old one.

Ragnarok: Ragnarok was the given name of the meteor the crashed into Earth on December 3, 2030. It was discovered by astronomer Neil Weinstein in 2019. Ragnarok was about three miles long, and two miles wide. It is not known how it eluded detection for so long.

Recon: A Recon is an all-terrain rover that is powered by hydrogen. It is designed for speedy recon missions across the Wastes, and was developed by the United States military during the Dark Decade. It is composed of a cab, in front, and a large cargo bay in the back. Mounted on top of the cargo bay is a turret with 360 degree rotation, accessible by a ladder and a porthole. The turret can be manned and fired while the Recon is on the go.

Wasteland, The: The Wasteland is a large tract of land comprising of Southern California and the Western United States. It extends from the San Bernardino Mountains in the west, to the Rockies in the east, and from the northern border of Mexico to the south, to the Ice Lands to the north (which is about the same latitude as Sacramento, California). The Wasteland is characterized by a cold, extremely dry climate. Rainfall each year is little to none, two to four inches being about average. Little can survive the Wasteland, meaning that all life has clung to limited water supplies. Major population centers include Raider Bluff, along the Colorado River, the settlement of Oasis, supplied by a body of water of the same name, and Last Town, a trading post that sprung up along I-10 between Los Angeles and the Mojave. Lost Angeles flanks the Wasteland's western extreme, while Las Vegas flanks its eastern extreme.

Wastelanders: Wastelanders are surface dwellers, specifically ones that live in the southwestern United States. The term is broad

– but generally it means a surface dweller who is forced to wander, scavenge, or raid for sustenance. Wastelanders are feared by Bunker dwellers, as they have been the number one reason for Bunkers failing.

Xenofungus: Xenofungus is a slimy, sticky fungus that is colored pink, orange, or purple (and sometimes all three). Whether benign or hostile, no one knows – and that is part of the focus of Dr. Steven Keener's research.

Xenovirus: The xenovirus is an agent that attaches itself to DNA, acquires it, and mixes and matches it with the DNA it has already collected. It mostly affects microbes, and more recently, plants, but it is thought to be benign.